A LOVE WORTH FIGHTING FOR: CANNON & TIFF

K. RENEE

Chapter One

CANNON

"**W**ho is it!" She yelled, swinging the door open with a scowl on her face.

"Damn, beautiful. You not happy to see me?"

"What are you doing here? Better yet, how the fuck do you know where I live?" I knew she was nervous by the way her voice trembled.

"I'm the man they call when a nigga needs to be found, finding you was a walk in the park. At least, I was nice enough to knock on the door, 'cause a nigga like me don't like doorbells or knocking. That shit is annoying as fuck. How many times did you think I was gone let your fine ass keep walking by me and not come for you and that sweet pussy you got between your thighs?" Pulling her into me, I could feel her body tense up under my touch. She was nervous, and that shit made me smile on the inside.

"You need to leave. I've told you dick is not what the fuck I'm-" I cut her off, lifting her up and pressing her against the door. Her breathing was short and erratic, and I was ready to tear lil' mama's life the fuck apart.

"I'm here to do one thing, and that's suck and fuck you until you can't scream my name no muthafuckin' more." I smiled.

"Pu...pu...put me down." She could barely get the words out, and all I could do was stare at her beautiful ass. Tiff was one of those women that you could look at, and your dick instantly got hard. Her caramel complexion, big ass, wide hips, and the sexiest mole right above her beautiful pouty lips; that shit was my weakness.

"The only time I'm putting you down is when you're sliding down on this dick. You may think you like pussy, but reality is about to fuck your life up, and that's on me."

"I...I can't do this...Ahhhhhhh!" She moaned as I slid my hand inside of her shorts, grazing my fingers across her fat ass pussy.

"If you want me to stop, I'll stop. The way this pussy soaking my fingers, I don't really think you want me to stop." I had to taste her. Pulling my fingers out of her and placing them in my mouth, licking her juices off, caused her to quiver. I could feel the fire building up inside of her, sliding my tongue across her lips was all it took. She sucked that mutha-fucka into her mouth like it was a vacuum. Nothing prepared me for the shit that happened next. Damn near ripping the clothes off of each other to get to what we both were starving for.

Sliding my dick back and forth across her wet pussy damn near made me nut prematurely. I knew then that I wasn't gone just be able to hit this shit one time and walk away. The moment I eased inside of her, she cried out like a wounded animal. I had to take it easy with her because I'm sure it had been a while since she had dick inside of her. Having a cannon inside of her can cause some serious fuckin' problems anyway. Once she adjusted to my size, she began moving up and down on my dick.

"Fuck!" I growled in her ear as my strokes went deeper and deeper into her walls. It was almost as if my movements were uncontrollable.

"Ohhhh, shit! I can't... I can't take it!" She moaned as she held on tighter.

"Girl, you gone take this dick and love that shit," I growled, deep-stroking the hell out of her.

"Cannon!" She cried out in ecstasy. That alone had me ready to tear her ass up and show her what the fuck she had been missing.

"What's up, beautiful? Just let me love on you tonight, and we can talk about that other shit in the morning. I want to show you what it's like to be with a real man, not some lil' boy that got you running from dick to suck on a clit. That shit ain't you, the way your pussy is gripping my dick right now. Your ass been waiting on the right dick to come along to show you some real shit, and I got you, baby." There was no way I was gone let her ass go after tonight. The days of her fucking with bitches were over.

"Fuck me! I need you to fuck me!" She moaned. Walking over to the couch with her in my arms, she eased down on my dick, gyrating up and down on my shit. The real Tiff showed up and showed the fuck out on this dick.

"The fuck!" I gritted as she started riding the tip of my dick and gripping my shit with her pussy muscles as she gyrated up and down on it. She repeated that shit for a while, and I swear a nigga was seeing stars. I have never been fucked like that before. Lil' mama and her pussy was gone be a problem for me and her.

"Mmmmm, shit! I'm cumming!" She screamed, but I couldn't form words to respond because the pussy was just that good. I just gripped her ass and fucked the cum right on out of her beautiful ass.

"Fuuuckkk! This pussy is beasting!" I came so damn hard my ass was shaking like a lil' bitch, and that's when I realized that I wasn't wearing a condom. Fucckkkk!

"Cannon! Cannon! I know damn well you didn't just call me your ex bitch name while the fuck I'm riding your mutha-fuckin' dick!" Dena yelled.

Fuck! I can't get this girl out of my fuckin' head. The whole time I was fucking, Dena, I was thinking about the first time I slid up in Tiff. She was already feeling some type of way about my relationship with Tiff.

"I don't know what the fuck you're talking about!" I said to her, knowing that I probably slipped the fuck up.

"Nigga, you know exactly what the fuck I'm talking about. I'm sick of this shit with you and that dyke ass bitch." She was going off, and I can understand her anger, but she gone watch her tone when she talking to me.

"Listen, my bad if that happened, but I don't recall saying no shit like that. I'm gone need you to watch your damn mouth with all that name calling. We not together. I'm fucking with you the long way, and I respect you, so I apologize if I said some off the wall shit. The pussy was feeling good and I guess I kind of blacked out." I got up and walked into the bathroom, leaving her standing there with her thoughts. It's clear that the shit with me and Tiff is unresolved. I have to do something about it because the shit was driving my ass crazy. It's been a year since I've seen her at Nas and Cas' wedding. That shit was fucking torture. It took everything in me not to walk up on her that day and squeeze the air out of her body.

That's a fucked up feeling to have about a woman that you would have given your life for, without thought. The moment I buried myself into her, pieces of her soul just seeped into my body and found it's resting place. I never expected to fall hard for her. It just happened, and now I'm regretting ever saying shit to her ass. Nas, Priest, and I have been friends for a long ass time, and I would hate to lose our friendship because I killed their cousin. So, the best thing for me to do is to stay the fuck away from her ass. I made this shit no secret on how I felt about the shit Tiff did to me. I hated saying her name because the shit left a bitter taste on my tongue.

When I stepped out of the shower and walked back into the bedroom, Dena was gone. I guess she mad. Her ass will be alright, and if not, oh well. I had been messing with her for a couple of years, but my mind wasn't right to make her my girl. Truth be told, my heart was fucked up, and I could never trust another woman. After Tiff and I got a taste of each other, that damn girl was on my dick every damn day for almost five months. She wasn't fucking with no other chicks; it was just me and her, and I honestly couldn't get enough of her. One day, I got a call from my brother's girl, letting me know that she thought she saw Tiff in the abortion clinic where she worked. She said she wasn't sure if that was her, so she took a picture and sent it to me. Sure enough, it was her ass. I asked her was she with somebody. She told me that Tiff was there to get an abortion, and hearing that shit caused me to black the fuck out! I was gone kill this bitch, and that was on my mama. I was so pissed I called Nas to let him know what the fuck was going on.

By the time I got dressed and got down to the clinic, it was too late. Tiff had already killed my fuckin' seed. She gave me this long, drawn out speech about her not being ready, and her life wasn't right to be bringing a kid into it. I would have respected her more if she told me about it, and we made decisions together. She could have had my damn baby, and I would have raised my child. I know it's her body, and ultimately, it would have been her choice, but damn lil' mama said fuck me. That shit was foul as fuck, and I just can't rock with her on that. If you woman enough to spread your legs without thought, be woman enough to give life if that ends up being your reality.

The only reason I didn't fuck her ass up is because of my friendship with her cousins and the fact that Nas pulled up at the clinic the same time I did. Best believe my gun was ready to do some muthafuckin' damage to her ass. I'm not the type of nigga that's gone play with yo' ass when it comes to me and mine. I had to have a drink just thinking about all the shit that went down with her. After I poured my drink, I walked back into the bedroom to get myself together for Nas & Cas' cookout today. Ever since I took over the operation, shit in my life changed for the good. I'm making more money than I've ever seen in my life and that shit felt good. The way I had shit setup, I barely touched the product or the streets. My team was solid, and my method in this game was A1. My phone was going off, and when I looked at it, I shook my head. I knew I was about to get my ass handed to me.

"What's up, Ma?" I asked her as I placed the call on speaker.

"Don't what's up me! Why the hell haven't I seen your ass in over a month? If I don't see you by tomorrow, I'm coming over there and fucking you up. I don't know what the fuck is wrong with you and your stupid ass brother. I have been calling y'all for the past week because your sister over here acting like I won't buss her ass down to the white meat!" She fussed.

"My bad, Ma, I will be over there tomorrow. Do you need anything?" I questioned, letting out an exasperated sigh.

"No, I just need to see my sons and for you to deal with your sister before I break my damn foot off in her ass," she spoke, and I couldn't help but chuckle. My mom and Mercedes were always going through some shit. We're all grown as hell, and my mom still thinks we are babies. Mercedes is twenty-five years old, my brother Shawn is twenty-Seven, and I'm twenty-nine. If it were left up to Brenda Mason, we would all still be living home with her.

"Ok, I will come by tomorrow, Ma, and I will bring Shawn with me." We spoke for a few minutes longer and then ended the call. Once I finished getting dressed, I grabbed my keys and headed out the door. It took me about twenty minutes to get to Nas' crib, and I could hear the music coming from the back of the house. I rang the bell, and a few minutes later, Cas opened the door.

"Hey, bro. Come on in." She smiled.

"What up? How was Paris?" I asked, kissing her cheek.

"I loved it. We were busy with all of the shoots Zoey had, but we found time to have some fun." She smiled. Cas managing Zoey was the move. Her management firm was growing, and Zoey just blew up with modeling, magazines, commercials, and she started her own clothing line.

"I'm glad you had a good time. Let me go out here and see what's up with your husband," I told her and walked out back.

"Nigga, I know yo' ass out here burning some shit up," I laughed, grabbing me a beer from the cooler.

"This gone be the best damn chicken yo' ass done ate in your life, and this sauce gone make you run and slap yo' mama. Wait. Not yo' mama, but it's gone make you slap another nigga's mama for real!" This dumb ass nigga said, and we burst out laughing.

"Who all coming over today?" I looked over at him.

"I wish you stop asking me that shit every time you come over here. You know damn well she lives in Cali, and if she comes to the city, I would have told you. Bruh, you gone have to let that shit go, nigga. How the hell can you move on if you still holding on to all that anger? I know the shit was fucked up, and I would feel the same way you do; it's been two years, and you gotta get right." Nas was right. I needed to let that shit go and forget her ass ever existed.

Chapter Two

TIFF

"Does Nas and Priest know you're home?" Brittany asked as we got in the car.

"No, I wanted to surprise them."

"Oh, they ass gone be surprised, alright." Brittany wasn't helping the situation at all. I was already nervous about how my cousins were going to react when they saw me. I haven't talked to them as much in the past year. Nas felt the need to keep talking shit to me about what I had done to Cannon. I made decisions that I would regret for the rest of my life, and I feel fucked about it. At the time, I was so lost. I wasn't ready to be a mother, and I didn't want to bring a baby into the crazy shit I had going on. I got so much grief from my family, it kind of pushed me away. Certain things that were happening in my life I kept to myself. I was hurt about how they treated me.

When Nas called and told me he and Cas were getting married, it took a lot for me to get on that plane and go to their wedding. I knew Cannon would be there, and I knew they would bring up what happened between us, and I was right. Once I got back to Cali, I didn't call as much. They looked down on me and didn't want to hear shit I had to say other than that I was wrong.

The look on Cannon's face when he came into that abortion clinic would forever be etched into my memory. Since I moved to California with Brittany, my life has changed in so many ways. Being with Cannon opened up something in me. It changed me, and the way I was living my life. I no longer wanted to be in a relationship with a woman. My desire to be with a man outweighed my desire to be with a woman. I guess I have Cannon to thank for that. I tried reaching out to him so many times to apologize, but he wanted nothing to do with me. Eventually, I respected his wish and moved on with my life.

"What did Marlo say about you coming to Philadelphia?" Brittany asked.

"He didn't like it, so he's flying out tomorrow." I looked over at her as I turned onto Nas' street. Marlo and I met a few months after I moved to Cali, and I've been with him for almost two years now. We got engaged about six months ago, and we have a beautiful daughter Aniya, that's four months old.

"That nigga better not come here acting like he some hard ass nigga. Your cousins gone humble his ass real quick! To be honest, I don't think it's the best time to introduce him to them. Especially with his controlling over the top ass." Brittany couldn't stand Marlo because she felt like he was too controlling and was trying to stop me from being friends with her. Brittany is my best friend; Marlo could never come between that, and he knew it. I pulled in front of Nas' house. There were a lot of cars here. We got out of the car and Brittany helped me with Aniya.

"Girl, I can't wait to see their damn face when they find out you had a baby," Brittany spoke as we rang the doorbell. It took a few minutes for someone to open the door.

"Tiff! What the hell! When did you come in town and who baby you got? Britt, you had a baby?" Nas questioned with a confused look on his face.

"Hell nawl! I don't believe in pushing nothing up out of this cat here. I got a virgin uterus, and we gone keep that shit that way," Britt blurted out.

"Nas, this is my daughter, Aniya," I said to him.

"Mmmm, mmmmm, nah! We not doing this shit today, this was supposed to be a good day and I live in a good damn neighborhood. I'm cool with the neighborhood captain, and I don't got time for the shit that's about to take place if you bring yo' ass up in here! The grim reaper is here, and his ass been killing niggas left and right for the last two years. Half the niggas he killed still asking why they the fuck dead! I would hate to see you be his next victim. This ain't it right now. Come back later when everybody is gone!" He said and slammed the door. I couldn't believe he did that shit. Brittany was bent over laughing so damn hard she was choking.

"Let's go, I think he means Cannon is here. I'm not ready to see him right now, and this isn't the best time for him to see my baby." Just as I turned to walk away, I heard Cas screaming.

"Ohhhh my God! Tiff, when did you get in town! Y'all come in, don't pay no attention to Nas dramatic ass," she yelled.

"I don't think it's a good idea, Cas," I told her.

"Why not? We haven't seen you in over a year. I should beat yo' ass for not calling me like you should. Awww, who's baby?" She questioned.

"This is my daughter, Aniya." I looked at her.

"What! You had a baby? Congrats, sis! Come on in... Ohhhh shit! We're having a cookout and Cannon is here," she spoke. "Maybe you should take yo' ass upstairs until we can figure out how to get his ass out of here."

"Cas, if you're letting her in the house, let me go get my damn gun first. I may have to shoot this angry nigga in the kneecaps, 'cause I damn sure won't be fighting his angry husky ass!" Nas yelled out from the door.

"Damn, that nigga still mad?! I will keep Niya with me, and you two niggas can fight this shit on out," Brittany dumb ass laughed.

"Bihhhh, you hold onto your baby. He won't touch you with her in your hand. Other than that, your ass might get it. Nas is right; Cannon has been on one since all that shit went down with you. But you can't run from him forever, and we're family. Your cousin is crazy as hell, and he may come down hard on you. I know for sure he would never let anything happen to you.

To be honest, I think Cannon still loves you, and what you did hurt him. I don't think he will hurt you. Let's go inside. Zoey is going to go crazy when she sees you." Cas attempted to grab the baby and thought about it. Brittany burst out laughing again, and we walked inside. I'm not sure if this was the best decision. I should have just left and come back later. I didn't want to hurt him any more than I already have. No one was inside the house. Everybody was out back, which gave me time to get myself together. Had I known they were having a cookout; I would have come by another time.

"I'm gone go scope out everything and let you know if it's safe to come out." Brittany shrugged and walked out back. I could hear Zoey scream because she knew if Brittany was here, then so was I. A few minutes later, Britt came running back in the house with Zoey behind her like they had fire attached to their ass.

"Get yo' shit, sis, Nas was right, this ain't it. Nas and Priest were talking to him, and that nigga straight turned into the Incredible Hulk. I don't think this is the time for you to be seeing him right now. As a matter of fact, I think you should just forget you ever knew that nigga," Britt spoke as she grabbed Niya's bag and pulling me to the door.

"As much as I want to catch up right now, Brittany is right. He is pissed, and I swear I would hate to cut his ass over you.

Tiff, she's beautiful. I'm mad as hell that you didn't tell us," Zoey said, hugging me.

"I'm sorry, I know I have a lot of explaining to do." Just as I said that Cannon came inside the house with Nas and Priest behind him.

"This is what the fuck you do! You go have a baby by the next nigga, but kill my fuckin' seed! Bi..... You ain't shit! Don't ever in your muthafuckin' life say shit to me again."

"Look, I know you mad, but you're not gone stand here and disrespect me. I'm sorry, and if I can go back in time, I wouldn't have done that. I don't regret having my daughter, and you're not gone make me feel bad for having her and bringing her around my family!" I cried because, at this point, I was pissed the fuck off. Wiping my eyes, I began patting Niya's back because she started crying.

"Oh my God! Tiff, you're married!" Zoey yelled out, and I forgot all about my engagement ring on my finger.

"What the fuck!" Cannon roared, punching a hole in the wall.

"Nigga! I know damn well you ain't punch up my shit! I'mma give you this one, but when you calm yo' overly hyper ass down, you gone fix my shit. Now I know shit is fucked up right now, but y'all gone have to talk this shit out. You're my bro and I know you pissed; just keep in mind that she's my cousin," Nas said to him, and he just walked out without saying shit to anyone. I handed Cas the baby, and I ran outside to try and talk to him. "Tiff, come back in here and talk to that nigga through the window!" I heard Nas yell out.

"Cannon! Please wait!" I called out.

"Nah, I'm good on you, lil' mama. Just stay the fuck away from me." He jumped in his car and sped out of the driveway. My heart felt like it was going to burst out of my chest. I never meant to hurt him this badly, and I don't know how to make it right. I love my fiancé and want him to meet my family, but Brittany was right. I don't think it's a good time for Marlo to come here.

"I can't believe this emotional ass nigga put a hole in my damn wall."

"Just call someone and get it fixed, babe," Cas spoke.

"Hell nawl! I'm not fixing that shit. When that nigga get right, he gonna bring his ass over here and patch my shit up. I knew we shouldn't have let Tiff ass in here until we got rid of that nigga."

"I can't believe she got married and didn't tell us," Zoey exclaimed.

"I didn't get married; I'm engaged," Tiff spoke, walking back into the room.

"Man, you need to sit your ass down and get to explaining. How did you get this baby? Did you go to one of them baby places and they put one in you?" She had my ass confused as hell.

"I'm engaged to my daughter's father. I'm not confused; I know what I want, and I'm in a happy place right now. I know what I did to Cannon was wrong, and I'm sorry about it. I tried apologizing to him, and he wouldn't hear me out. He wanted nothing to do with me, so I moved on with my life. I regret what I did, but I can't stop living. I do want to be in a good space with my family. It seems that you all turned against me for the decisions I made back then," she cried, and I felt fucked up about it.

"I didn't mean to make you feel that way. I wasn't feeling your decision, but I would never turn my back on you, Tiff. We're gone always be family, and that trumps everything and anybody. Now, get your confused ass over here and give me a hug." We all burst out laughing.

"Yeah, no matter what the circumstances are, we got you," Priest said, pulling her in for a hug.

"What's up with this dude you're about to marry?" I asked her.

"His name is Marlo; he will be here tomorrow. I want y'all to meet him, so maybe we can all hang out at the club tomorrow night?" She stated.

"Whew, this about to be a mess," Brittany mumbled, and I caught that shit.

"Yeah, we can do that," I told her.

"Tiff, she is so beautiful," Zoey said, taking the baby from Cas.

"Thank you, I love her entire existence. I never knew I could love unconditionally until I held her in my arms. What y'all got to eat in here, I'm hungry?" She smiled, walking into the kitchen.

"I see that shit ain't changed about yo' greedy ass!" We all burst out laughing. For the rest of the night, we got caught up on everything that was happening with all of us.

———

I was on my way over to check on Cannon. I knew he was still feeling some type of way about him and Tiff. I just didn't know the shit was still fuckin' with him like that. I rang the doorbell waiting for him to open the door.

"Sup?" He allowed me in, and we walked into his family room.

"I wanted to come check on you. Shit was crazy yesterday. Bro, I didn't know she was coming home, and I damn sure didn't know she had a baby." The look this nigga gave me let me know that maybe I should just shut the fuck up.

"I can't even tell you what's going through my head right now. I mean, this girl killed my baby just to go get pregnant by another nigga and have his kid. And then she goes and marries the nigga. That shit got me ready to murder a nigga!" He roared.

"Bruh, she's not married yet, and before she does get married, I think you two should talk. You need to get some shit off yo' chest and either close the book or open that muthafucka back up. Because you clearly still love her, a blind man can see that shit." I shrugged, getting up to go pour me a drink from the bar.

"I don't love shit! I know that's your cousin, so it's best that we stop talking about the shit. I'm good on her, and anything about her ass. Keep that shit to yourself. Our shipment is coming in, and I'm about to head out and make sure everything is good. Did the repairman come through and fix your wall?" He asked.

"Yeah. Nigga, next time tear your own shit up. Don't bring yo' angry ass over to my crib fuckin' up my good shit. You can say what you want, but I know you feeling something for my cousin with yo' mad ass! I'm glad we had this talk, I'mma head out and get shit ready at the club for tonight. Oh yeah, I guess I'll keep that her nigga is here, and they gone be at the club tonight to myself. Since yo' mad ass don't give a damn. Thought maybe you wanted to come scope out your competition 'cause this shit with you and Tiff ain't over." I dapped his angry bird looking ass up and left out. By the time I made it back home, it was almost nine.

"Babe, I'm riding with you to the club tonight. I want to get my drink on, and I can't do that if I have to drive. I'm just gone catch a ride home with Zoe and Priest if you're going to close up tonight." Cas walked up, kissing my lips.

"Nah, I'm not closing. We supposed to be hanging out with Tiff and her dude. I can't believe her ass done had a baby and talking about marrying that nigga. Ion like dude already; her ass supposed to be with Cannon. I know she fucked up; I just think it's still some hope for them." Cannon can say what he wants, but I know what it is with him.

"Nas, you haven't met the guy yet," she laughed.

"Cas, Ion like him, and yo' ass better not like him neither. We team Cannon over here. Fuck dude!" I shrugged, putting my shoes on so we could leave.

"Damn right, fuck dude! So, we gone help them rekindle and pray he can forgive her for what she did to him. Operation get Tiff and Cannon back together is in full effect." She smiled, and I had to press pause on her ass.

"Mmmm, mmm, hell nawl! I'm not playing no damn matchmaker and shit. The last time we did that shit, that took all my energy, and I had to practice my lines just so the shit would come outright. And Cannon is a different type of damn animal than Priest was. This nigga is a walking time bomb; anything can set him off at this point. I did put a bug in his ear about tonight, though. I doubt he comes since he ain't fucking with Tiff," I told her.

"What! What if he decides to come?" She questioned.

"That nigga ain't coming, now bring your fine ass on. Since our son is with your mom, I'mma tear yo' ass up when we get back home tonight." Cas' mom took us up on our offer, so I built her a two-bedroom guest house out back and she loves it. We love having her here to help us with our son, and the best part is she cooks for my ass errrday.

"I got that good-good for you, zaddy. We gone be swinging from the ceiling tonight!" I looked over at her crazy ass and burst out laughing. About thirty minutes later, we were walking into the VIP section of my club. Tiff, Brittany, and I guess the dude they were talking too was her fiancé, was sitting at the bar.

"What's up?" I greeted, walking up to them.

"Hey, cousin. Where are Zoe and Priest?" Tiff asked as she stood hugging Cas and me.

"I thought he would be here by now," I said to her, looking in the direction of the dude sitting with them.

"Nas, Cas, this is my fiancé Marlo. Bae, this is my cousin Nas and his wife Cas," Tiff introduced us.

"Sup, nice spot you have here," Marlo spoke as he dapped me up.

"'Preciate that, man. Ayee, Shana, drinks are on the house for them!" I yelled over the music to my barmaid, as Cas and I took a seat at the bar. **Go Crazy by Chris Brown** came blaring through the speakers, and the ladies jumped up dancing and acting crazy like old times.

"Tiff, you good. Sit down!" Marlo grabbed her arm and pulled her back in her seat. My bitch nigga monitor instantly went off with his ass.

"Damn, I'm just trying to chill and have a good time with my family. I'm not about to be sitting here in a chair all night babysitting you," Tiff bellowed, and she got back up to dance with the girls while this nigga had his face all balled the fuck up. A few minutes later, Priest and Zoe came walking in and greeted us.

"Bout time y'all got here," I told them.

"We all know how my wife is when she's getting dressed," Priest acknowledged, smiling over at Zoe.

"Whatever!" Zoey laughed, nudging him.

"Yo, you the modeling chick, right? I've seen you on TV and in magazines," Marlo said to Zoe, which caused Priest to turn to him quick as hell. He better tread softly fuckin' with that nigga and his wife.

"Priest, Zoey, this is my fiancé Marlo," Tiff introduced.

"Babe, look," Cas whispered in my ear, nudging the hell out of my arm. Looking at what she was looking at caused me to shake my damn head. I knew tonight was getting ready to be a muthafuckin' massacre when Cannon and his brother Shawn stepped into the VIP.

Chapter Four

CANNON

Finding out Tiff had a baby fucked me up, but I'm the type of nigga that don't let shit die easily. The fact that she felt the need to bring this nigga to my city didn't sit well with me. I always come to the club on the weekends, and that shit ain't gone stop now because she got her nigga with her.

"Bruh, if this nigga gets sideways, just know I'm knocking his head off, and he can pick that shit up and take it back to Cali with him," Shawn spoke. It seems that all eyes were on me, and Tiff ass looked like her ass was ready to make a run for it.

"Not if I do that shit first," I said to him as we approached the bar.

"What's up?" I dapped Nas and Priest up and hugged all of the ladies, except Tiff.

"Shana, let me get my usual and send it over to the section." There was no way that I was gone sit at the bar.

"How you been, Cannon?" Britt asked.

"I'm good, what about you?" I looked over at her.

"Bro, I'm going over to the section," Shawn stated as Britt looked him up and down.

"Damn, they're making y'all Philly niggas finer and finer every time I come here! Maybe I need to move my ass back to indulge." Britt smiled at him.

"You don't want to climb this tree, lil' baby. I'm not your typical nigga. I will fuck the shit out of you without thinking twice, and your ass will definitely be moving back to Philly." He winked at her and walked off. I had to laugh because Britt needs to think about her next move and make it her best move fuckin' with that crazy nigga. I decided to be a messy nigga and speak to Tiff.

"What's up, Tiff?" She looked at me in surprise knowing I didn't fuck with her.

"Hey, Cannon. This is-" I cut her off.

"I'm good, lil' mama, I'm not interested in knowing who this nigga is. I just didn't want to be rude and not speak to you." I smirked at her.

"Ahhh, hell! Y'all be ready for whatever at this point." Nas was right. They needed to get ready because I was on one, and this nigga could get it.

"Periodt! But I'm here for it, talk yo' shit, Cannon," Britt spat, and Tiff rolled her eyes at her.

"Bruh, when you talking to my girl, you gone know me,"

her bitch made nigga spoke. I knew I was in the wrong, but who gives a fuck. I said what the fuck I said, I say what I want and do what I want.

"The only person I need to know is her, and I clearly know her from the inside out." I smirked.

"My nigga!" Nas blurted out.

"Ummmm, Cannon, don't do that." I could tell that Tiff was nervous, so I let the shit go and turned to leave. That is until the next thing that came out his nigga mouth halted my steps.

"So, that's the nigga you was fuckin' and killed his kid. Obviously, the pussy still got an issue, but I'm gone solve that muthafucka for him. Get your shit and let's go. Got me in here going back and forth with this bitch ass nigga. She killed your kid because she was waiting on me, nigga!" That shit had me on this nigga before he could blink. I tried to rip this nigga muthafuckin' head off.

"What the fuck you say, bitch!" I roared, punching his ass over and over again. He was trying to get his shit off, but I had erupted, and there was no match for the shit I was giving this pussy. I could hear the screaming and yelling, but my ass was zoned out, and all I wanted was this nigga in a body bag. Security tried to pull me off of him, and I wasn't having it.

"Nah, don't nobody touch him! That nigga deserve this muthafuckin' beat down. He could have said anything else, but that bullshit!" Nas roared.

"Cannon! Stop it! You're going to kill him!" Tiff screamed, and that was exactly what I was trying to do, kill his ass.

"Come on, bro!" I heard Nas say as they pulled me off him. The nigga was still on the floor when my brother kicked him in his shit. Security helped Tiff get his pussy ass off the floor and took him out of the club. I swear that nigga was lucky they were still holding me down.

"Fucccckkkkkkkk!" I roared.

"You good?" Priest asked.

"Man, I'm ready to kill that nigga. I know she got a baby by him, and I know I started the shit, but I'm ready to murder that nigga."

"Yeah, that was fucked up," Priest stated, just as Nas came walking up.

"Come outside with me for a minute," he said, and I followed him out. When we made it outside, we heard yelling coming from the parking lot.

"You think that shit cute, you out here taking up for this nigga!" The guy yelled.

"Your ass was wrong; you knew that situation was sensitive for both of us. Yet when you realized who he was, you threw the shit in his face. Yeah, he said some crazy shit to you. You could have just kept that shit gutter and talked your shit. What you said was fucked up and you know it. The fuck!" Tiff yelled. I knew that voice from anywhere.

"Bitch, I will break your fuckin' jaw out here! I'm the only nigga you gone go hard for!" He told her, and Nas and I were already walking up on them.

"Nah, you not talking to my cousin like that, bruh! I will murder yo' ass and send you back to your mama in a pine fuckin' box. We don't play them type games. Now y'all can handle yo' personal business, but if you put your hands on her, I'm coming for you. You a foul ass nigga for what the fuck you said, and you deserved what the fuck you got! If you feel like you need to get some of that muthafuckin' aggression off of you, I can give you what you're looking for! I can't stand niggas like you. Tiff, Ion like yo' dude, and that's that on that!" Nas said to them.

"Nigga, fuck you!" Before Nas could react, I was punching that nigga in his fuckin' jaw again. When I said every time I see his ass, I meant that shit! Security came running over and pulled me off of him, and Tiff was standing there in tears.

"Tiff, you good?" Nas asked her as they pulled me away.

"Yeah, I'm sorry about all of this. It was supposed to be a fun night," she spoke, wiping her tears away. I was ready to explode in this parking lot. I had to get the fuck out of here. The rest of the crew was already outside.

"Bro, lets ride!" I told my brother.

"Lil' mama, you coming with me?" Shawn asked Britt, and she nodded that she was.

"Tiff, I'm going with Shawn, I will see you tomorrow," Brittany said to her. Walking to the car, I couldn't stop the rage inside of me. That shit was boiling over, and there wasn't a damn thing nobody could do about it. I had so many unanswered questions, and at this point, I didn't give a damn who that nigga was to her. I turned, walking back over to where they all were standing. I picked Tiff's ass up, placing her over my shoulders, and walked back to my car.

"Cannon, put me fuckin' down! Are you crazy!" She screamed.

"The last time you told me to put you down, you landed on my dick. Tonight is no fuckin' different!"

"Yooooo, that nigga is a straight-up savage! Nigga, you just gone let him take yo' girl like that?!" I heard Nas yell out.

"Bro, I need you to drive my car and drop me off home." I threw him the keys and put her in the car. She was still going off, trying to get her ass out. She was coming with me, and I didn't give a fuck about her doing all that damn screaming. We all hopped in, and Shawn pulled off, headed to my crib.

Chapter Five

TIFF

I can't believe that he just did that shit. How the fuck am I going to explain being snatched up by the next nigga. As soon as I saw Cannon walking into the club, I knew it was going to be some shit. I'm pissed the hell off that Marlo did that shit, but Cannon is so fuckin' wrong right now. About twenty minutes later, we were pulling in front of a house that I've never seen before, so I assumed Cannon moved.

"Let's go." He looked over at me.

"Cannon, I'm not going inside. I have a fiancé, and this shit is fuckin' disrespectful," I argued.

"You're going in one of two ways; you can walk in or I will carry you in." He got out of the car, walked to my side, and opened the door.

"Bye, sis. Make sure that nigga hit it from all angles!" Britt yelled out, and I wanted to slap the shit out of her ass. The next thing I knew, I was being lifted out of the seat. As soon as he closed the door, Shawn backed out of the driveway. He carried me inside, walking upstairs to his bedroom and placing me on my feet.

"Why did you do that shit? Marlo is going to lose his damn mind!" I snapped as soon as he put me down. He just stared at me with this look that made me nervous as hell.

"Do me a favor. Don't speak on that nigga when you with me. I poured my fuckin' soul out to you, and you go do some fuck shit by killing my fuckin' baby. Why didn't you come to me, Tiff?! Why would you go and do some shit like that and then come back here like shit is all good with another nigga's baby? You don't see anything wrong with that shit!" He roared, his eyes were bloodshot red, and he was damn near foaming at the mouth. The way he was looking made me feel like total shit, and I couldn't stop the tears from flowing down my face.

"Cannon, I'm so sorry. It was such a bad mistake, and I will have to live with that for the rest of my life. I never meant to hurt you and it was selfish of me to make that decision on my own. I promise you if I could go back in time, I wouldn't have done that. Back then, I was going through so much that you didn't know about, and I wasn't in a good space to have a baby."

"Don't give me that bullshit excuse! I would have taken my fuckin' kid!" He yelled as tears began to fill the rim of his eyes. I stepped closer to him, placing my hand on his face.

"I'm sorry, I don't know what else to do or say to make this situation better. I can't be here with you. I'm engaged to someone else," I whispered. I truly didn't want to have an attitude with him, nor did I want to make matters worse. I know things were different with us, but I still wanted to have some type of closure with him.

"So, you really love this nigga?" He asked, never breaking his stare.

"Yes, I love him." He chuckled, and the way he was watching me let me know that my answer triggered some shit in him. I almost felt like I needed to get the fuck out of here. Fuck that! I know I need to get the fuck out of here. Just as the thought crossed my mind, he pulled me closer to him, crashing his lips onto mine. I tried to push him back, but the way he was sucking on my bottom lip had my ass stuck, and my hoes ass pussy twitching like the bitch was fighting an addiction. I couldn't hold it. I have missed this man and yearned for him for so fucking long. We were so fucking hungry, clothes were being ripped apart, and when his tongue touched my body, I was on fire. He skillfully sucked and licked from my neck to my breasts, sliding his finger onto my pussy as he massaged my clit. A moan escaped my mouth, and that was all he needed to hear. He lifted me in the air like I was a sheet paper, placing me on top of his dresser. When he turned the soundbar on *Again by DVSN Ft. Shantel* came on, and my heart felt like it was going to explode.

"Fuck! You wet!" He growled in my ear.

"Cannon, please!" I called out. I felt like my breath got

caught in my throat when he slammed his big ass dick inside of me without warning.

"Is this what you want, 'cause I got two years of reserved fucking to get off my muthafuckin' chest?" The more he talked his shit, the wetter I got. His thrusts became deeper and deeper, and I was doing my best to keep up. His thrusts were so powerful it brought tears to my eyes. It was like we were both fighting to be in this moment, and it still wasn't enough. I knew all of this shit was wrong, but there was no way that I could stop.

"Gotdamn, this pussy is a muthafucka!" He slammed into me over and over again, pounding on my g spot. I have never been fucked this hard and good in my damn life. I was losing it, and there was nothing I could do about it as cum began pouring out of me.

"Ohhh... Oh, fuck! Cannon! Fuck this pussy harder!" I screamed.

"Fuck! Give me that shit, lil' mama, cause... Ahhhhhhhh! Fuck!" He roared as I clamped down on his dick and started throwing and grinding my pussy on his ass. He pulled out of me and flipped me over, entering me from behind and fucking my life up. I don't remember this nigga dick being this damn good. He was fucking me so damn hard I could feel that shit in my chest, and he had my ass running.

"Oh my God!" I screamed as I tried to get him to ease up a little.

"Stop fuckin' running and take this muthafucka! Talking 'bout you love that nigga! Your pussy is wrapped around my dick, you gone love this dick and everything that comes with that shit!" He gritted as he gripped my ass, thrusting into me so damn deep, I couldn't even respond to what he was saying. This shit felt good as hell, but it also felt like he was giving me 'Bitch, I'mma fuck yo' ass up' strokes. Pulling out of me, he sat down on the bed and pull me on top of him.

"Ahhhhhhh, shit!" I moaned as I eased down on him.

"Damn! This pussy is a fuckin' beast," He gritted, slamming me down on his dick, fucking the shit out of me. I tried to keep up, but this nigga was just too much for me to handle.

"Mmmmm, shit! I can't hold it... Oh Godddd! I'm cumming!" I screamed as I began squirting all on his dick.

"That's what the fuck I'm talking about! I love a sloppy wet pussy... Argghhhhhhh, fuckkkkkk!" He growled, gripping my ass cheeks as he came with me. We just laid there in our thoughts, until he eased out of me and got out of bed.

"Get cleaned up, and I will take you back to your man." As soon as the shit rolled off his tongue, I felt like shit. A couple hours later, he dropped me off in front of my mother's house.

"I will call you later." He nodded and I got out of the car. My rental car was in the driveway, and I knew it was going to be some shit. Taking a deep breath, I rang the doorbell, because I didn't have my key or phone to call my mom. When Cannon snatched me up, I had already put my purse in the car. My mom opened the door, shaking her head.

"Girl, what in the flying fuck did you get yourself into? This crazy looking nigga been walking around here, acting like a plum fool. Talking to himself and shit, you know I don't do crazy. And who the fuck beat his ass black and blue, and took yo' ass?

"Cannon."

"Lawwd, I see why there was nothing he could do to stop it. Done let Cannon's fine ass come in and just take his girl! In his face! That's some hard shit right there. That's the kind of nigga I need just come in and take what you want," she laughed, shaking her head.

"Ma, where is Aniya?" I wanted to make sure my baby was good.

"She's in my room asleep for now. I told his ass if he keeps doing all that damn yelling he would be on the other side of the door," she spoke just as Marlo walked into the living room.

"You think this shit sweet? I'm got something for that nigga! You just gone ride off with that nigga and leave me in a fuckin' parking lot. I'm gone see that nigga; this shit is not over. It's damn near six in the morning, and you walking in here like you weren't with another nigga. Did you fuck him?!" He roared, looking like a mad man, gripping me by the neck and pushing me up against the wall. **Whap!** I slapped the shit out of his ass for putting his hands on me. He has a right to be mad, but nah, I'm the wrong bitch to be putting his hands on.

"Don't get fucked up in here. Make that the last time you touch me. You can say what the fuck you have to say without putting your hands on me." This nigga had me pissed the hell off.

"Nigga, you done lost all the mind the devil gave yo' ass! If you ever put your hands on my child again, I promise you that's gone be the last time you use that bitch," my mom told him.

"Pack your shit, we're going back home!" He stated, ignoring what my mom said, but he damn sure stepped away from me.

"I'm here visiting my mom for a week; I'm not leaving just because you're in your feelings. I didn't ask you to come here. You came because you wanted to control my every move," I told him.

"What I don't understand is, how you let another nigga walk off with your fiancé? That just don't sit right with me." My mom was not helping this situation at all with her crazy ass.

"Mom, I'm good. Why don't you go back to bed?" I said to her. When she left the room, I walked upstairs to my bedroom, with Marlo still going off behind me.

"Tiff, you didn't answer my fuckin' question. Did you fuck him?" He looked over at me. I didn't want to lie to him, but there was no way that I could tell him that Cannon had his big, beautiful fuckin' dick so far in me that I could feel that shit lodged in my throat. And the fucked-up thing is all I could think about is him right now. Visions of him sliding in and out of me were taking over and had my pussy pulsating. Fuckkkkk! This shit could not be happening to me right now.

"Answer my damn question!" He yelled, jolting me out of my thoughts.

"No," I blurted out and walked into the bathroom.

"Tiff, I'm not playing. We're going back to Cali as soon as I can get us a flight." I knew he was serious about going home; I'm just not going with him.

"I told you I'm not leaving. It's been a year since I've seen my family and my mom is bonding with her granddaughter. If you want to go, you can, just know that I'm staying. I'm sorry this happened, Marlo. I think you should calm down and let's enjoy our time here. You won't have to worry about my cousins or Cannon anymore. One more thing, don't ever make the mistake of putting your hands on me again." I wanted him to know that I'm not playing no games with his ass. He got a problem if he thinks we gone be on that type of time.

"I'm not worried about them niggas; they gone see me about this shit. My bad for doing that shit to you. You know how I get when I feel disrespected. I have to leave in a couple of days anyway, so I will stay until then. I need some pussy. It's been a long night." I had to think fast because I couldn't fuck him.

"I told you yesterday that I was cramping, my cycle came on. Marlo, I think it's best that you leave it alone when dealing with my cousins. I know you're in the streets and got your crew, but don't start a war with my family. I won't let you hurt them, and I'm not going to let them hurt you. You all were wrong for disrespecting each other, and I plan on talking to them about it. I'm begging you to just leave the shit alone. Have you seen my purse? I need to get my phone out of it?" I had to try and change the subject quickly.

"I hear you. Your purse is in the car. I'm going to bed. I'm tired as hell," he said, and I was so thankful that he was dropping this shit for now. I knew he was mad, but at least, he calmed down. Walking out of my room, I went out to the car and grabbed my purse. My phone had a few missed calls from Cas, and Nas. I had a text message from a number I didn't recognize.

Unknown: *You better not fuck that nigga! I don't give a damn what he is to you.*

Me: *Who the fuck is this?*

Unknown: *Stop fuckin' playing with me.*

Oh, my God, how did Cannon get my damn number? I thought. I'm going to fuck Brittany up. I know she gave him my shit. What the hell have I gotten myself into?

Chapter Six

BRITTANY

I'm being the biggest hoe right now, and I'm loving every minute of my hoeness. The shit that got me screaming inside is the way Cannon beat the breaks off Marlo ass. Wheeew. Baby, I've been waiting on this day to come ever since I met his pussy ass. I can't stand Marlo's ass. That nigga ain't shit. I tried to tell Tiff the nigga was full of shit. I've caught that nigga staring at me plenty of times. I don't want to start no shit with my best friend and having her think that I want her man.

"You good?" Shawn asked, walking into the bedroom with his dick swinging.

"I'm tired as hell, but I'm definitely good." I smiled at him when he climbed back into bed. This nigga fucked me so good my fuckin' uterus was clapping. I needed to be dicked down. It's been two months since I had some damn dick. I have never gone that long without having sex. So, getting with this sexy ass man was much needed, and ion even care that I just met his ass. 'Cause Laaawd, this nigga is finnneeee. His tannish brown complexion, brown eyes, tattoos, and oh my God, the muscles on his ass just set everything off about him. He had the prettiest set of white teeth, and his hair was faded around the sides with a curly coiled fro. God bless they mama because she did her thing when she had them. Cannon was even finer than his damn brother, and Marlo ass can't even compare. His ass can't even sit at the table with Cannon on his bad day.

"Nah, ain't no sleep going on in here, shorty. You talked all that shit, now we gone fuck until I pull all that cum out of you. When it comes to some good pussy, I don't get tired. That shit fuels me." He pulled me on top of him, sliding his fingers over my clit, causing my pussy to jump.

"Sssssssss, fuck!" I moaned as I grinded my pussy on his fingers.

"Damn, girl, you wet as fuck!" He spoke, grabbing a condom from the nightstand and moving me a little to sheath his dick.

"Get on that mufucka and ride that shit," he spoke as my cell phone started going off on his nightstand. I glanced at it, and this nigga picked it up to answer it.

"You worry about riding my dick, and I'm gone worry about this nigga Tre that's calling you early in the fuckin' morning."

"Yo, what up?" he spoke into the phone and I was about to

shit! Tre was my ex. We had been talking for the past couple of weeks trying to decide if we were gone try to work shit out. I guess that shit isn't going to happen now.

"Who the fuck is this? Yo, put Britt on the phone, nigga!" Tre barked.

"Nah, Britt can't come to the phone right now, playboy. She a lil' busy trying to pull this nut up out of me. And do me a favor. Stop calling her damn phone so fuckin' early in the morning. Fuckkkk! Ride that shit, lil' mama," he gritted, ending the call and throwing my phone on the bed.

I know I should be pissed about what he just did, but for some reason, that shit turned me the fuck on. He started fucking me so good a bitch was shedding some tears. Ion know if I like that type of dick, dick like that can make you lose your damn mind. He flipped me over and was pounding the fuck out of my pussy. If I ain't neva been fucked like this before in my life was a person, that hoe would be me! Damn! He turned me over and slid in from behind. This nigga slammed in me so hard my ass almost went flying across the room.

"Lil' mama, let me tell you something this pussy...*Whap!* Is. *Whap!* Fya. *Whap!* As. *Whap!* Fuck! *Whap!*" He roared, and that shit did it for me. With him smacking and pounding my ass, I was leaking like a faucet.

"Shit! On God! I'm cummingggggg! Ohhhh fuck! I'm cumming so hard! I think you broke my pussy 'cause it won't stop!" I screamed so damn loud; you would've thought this nigga was killing me.

"Nahhh, I didn't break it. I fucked it how it should be fucked, lil' baby! Argghhhhh! Fuck, this some good pussy!" He growled as he let loose in the condom. A few minutes later, we got up and took a shower. I was so damn tired. I knew I was going to sleep the day away.

"Oh yeah, cancel that nigga," he spoke, pulling me into him. I didn't respond, but I damn sure heard him. Damn, I love me a thugged out, rude ass nigga.

"*H*ey, babe. Where are you headed?" She asked, kissing my lips.

"Sup, I'm headed over to Priest house. The new cook started this morning. Bear, what the hell you cooking?" I peeped over her shoulder to see what the hell she had going on. My bear was putting in the effort to try and cook, but her ass just ain't there yet. Even though I had my mother in-law cooking for me now, I still miss my girl, Ms. Carol. There will never be another one like her. Her husband decided to retire and move in the house in Florida that we bought him. Before he left, he dropped off a book of recipes of hers, and I've been doing a lil' cooking myself.

"I'm making you some eggs and bacon. I didn't know you were going over there." She pouted.

"Hell yeah, I need to see what type of skills her ass got. I

called Zoey and put my request in for lunch. I'm gone eat
your food too since you worked so hard to cook it," I told her
as I sat down at the table.

"Babe, that shit was crazy last night. I still can't believe
how bad Cannon beat that boy ass, and he was still talking
shit."

"She can't bring that nigga around us, and I feel bad that
she's in a fucked-up position like that. Priest isn't feeling his
ass, and neither am I. That nigga lucky I didn't put his ass in
the dirt last night. The only reason he still breathing is
because of Tiff and her daughter," I spoke as she placed my
breakfast in front of me. These cheese eggs and bacon looked
good as hell, that was until I put the shit in my mouth.

"Bear, what the fuck is going on with these damn eggs!
This shit taste like ass and cheap ass at that!" I looked at her
ass with my face all damn twisted. Her ass burst out laughing.
I done had my share of bad ass and this shit taste just like it.

"Boy, ain't shit wrong with them eggs. I used a lil' bit of
this oil and scrambled them up for you," she laughed.

"Bruh, ion want that shit! I'm scared to even try this
bacon. Fuck that! I'm 'bout to go get my ass something to eat.
Whatever the fuck you did don't do that shit no mo'. Bring
your ass on if you coming with me 'cause I ain't bringing you
no damn plate back."

"That's fucked up, Nasir. You shouldn't talk about my food
like that," she laughed.

"What's fucked up is that you tried to feed me that nasty
shit." I grabbed my keys and headed for the door. I bet by the

time I got to the car, her ass was walking out the door because she knew she wasn't eating that shit she cooked. For old time's sake, I sent Tiff a text to let her know that Priest and Zoe got a new cook, and she better bring that ass. I told her to leave her nigga if she wanted him untouched.

"Ma and Omari must be having a good time. I called to check on him, and she said that he was staying over with her, and she wasn't cooking this weekend." She shrugged as I pulled out of the driveway.

"Ion know if building her that guest house out back was a good idea, 'cause her ass done got too comfortable back there. I've been contemplating on burning it down and just telling her we can't rebuild it." I was serious as hell, and Bear was about to cough up a damn lung, she was laughing so hard.

"Boy, you need Jesus. You can't burn down my mama shit because you want her to move in with us. Who are you, and where the fuck did you come from?" She asked, shaking her head at me. Pulling into Priest's driveway, we got out and walked inside, heading straight to the kitchen. When we walked in, Zoey was feeding their daughter Marley and talking to Big Mama, while Lil Priest was eating and playing with Sash. Zoey took this motherhood thing serious, and she didn't play about her kids. Shit, when she had Marley, she had to put her foot down with my brother 'cause that crazy nigga was trying to have another damn baby. I'm cool on that shit; my damn son was enough for right now.

"Boy, sit yo' ass down and tell me what happened last night. I called your ass after Zoey tried to give me the lowdown, but this heifer act like she can't tell a story right," Big Mama spoke while she fucked that damn food up she was eating.

"Uncle Nasir! Come sit by me," Sash said with excitement. That lil' girl was something else. She was growing up and so beautiful.

"Ok, baby, give me a minute. I need to fix me a plate." That shit looked good as hell. I saw the new cook placing more food on the bar. She looked as if she was a tad bit younger than Ms. Carol. I looked at my wife, and her damn plate was so full, the shit was about to fall off.

"Bear, where my plate at?" I asked her, shaking my head.

"Over there on the damn rack, nigga. This shit looks good, bae. You better make sure you get you some of these mixed greens and cabbage. I tasted a lil' bit of those and lawd, they melt in your damn mouth," Cas greedy ass spoke. Ion know if I'm feeling how they acting over her damn food, disrespecting my OG Ms. Carol like that. Fuck that! This her kitchen and Addie better recognize that shit.

"The test gone be how she takes to me and what this food talkin' 'bout. If shit don't work for me, we gone have to let her ass go," I whispered to Cas.

"Babe, how you gone come up in here talking about, we gone have to let her go? This ain't our house and you can't fire her," Cas was laughing, but I was serious as hell.

"You must be Nasir, I'm Addie. Ms. Zoey told me that I had to take extra care of you and to make sure I cooked whatever you needed. I made all of your favorites, as she requested, and I hope you enjoy them. Let me know if there is anything else I can get for you. She also told me you were very close to Ms. Carol and I want you to know that I will never try to take her place."

"Nah, you could nevaaa do that, and I'm glad we have that understanding. How you doing, though? A lil' advice be careful around these parts. Did they tell you where Ms. Carol is and how she got there? If I was you, I wouldn't agree to cook at nobody else house other than this one." I smiled at her and proceeded to fix my plate. If she knew like I did, she would go get her ass a gun and carry that shit around in her apron.

"Nasir!" Zoe and Cas yelled out.

"What! She needs to be careful fuckin' with this family!" I shrugged and finished fixing my plate.

"It's ok, I already know everything. Mr. Priest and Mrs. Chamber didn't leave anything out." She smiled and patted me on the arm.

"Boy, hurry up and get yo' ass situated and tell me what went on at the club," Big Mama fussed.

"Ma, Tiff is engaged, and she wanted us to meet her fiancé. Well, the nigga seemed like he controls that situation they got, and he disrespectful as fuck. I mean, Cannon was giving his ass attitude, but so the fuck what, that's just who Cannon is. The fucked-up thing about it is the nigga threw up the abortion shit in Cannon's face, and my nigga went beast mode on his ass. This nigga said fuck it, snatched Tiff ass up, and walked away with her ass. That shit was the best part of the night. He watched his girl get carried off by a mutha-fuckin' boss and couldn't do shit about it. Damn! This chicken slammin'!" I said as I bit down on another piece.

"Mmmm, hmmmm, taste the damn mac & cheese, bae," my greedy ass wife spoke with a mouthful of food. I think I might like Lil Ms. Addie. I'mma need to feel her out and see how shit goes.

"Lord have mercy, that damn Cannon is something else! Well, have y'all check on Tiff to see if her ass was alive? We all know Cannon ass got a screw missing. It's always the fine ones that will get your ass caught up." Just as Big mama asked that question, Tiff came walking in with her daughter.

"Hey, y'all," she spoke, placing the seat down, pulling Aniya out and passing her to Big Mama.

"The fuck wrong with you? You look like you walked through the gates of hell and the devil spit yo' ass back out!" I spoke and everyone fell out laughing.

"Bruh, I haven't been to sleep, and I can't sleep right now. I'm hungry as hell, though, and this food smells amazing," she stated, walking over to the food bar, and it look like her ass was limping. I'm glad Zoe took the kids to the playroom 'cause a nigga want to know what went down after her ass was snatched up.

"Tiff, this lil' doll looks just like you. I should beat your ass for not keeping in touch with us," Big Mama told her.

"I'm sorry, ma. It won't happen again," she said to her as she walked back to the table.

"Bruh, why the hell you limping like that? That nigga put

his hands on you?" I asked with my face frowned up because today would be a good day to kill a nigga.

"No, my legs are just a little sore." Is all she said.

"Lawd, you done slid down on the devil's dick. I know that type of walk from anywhere. I may be older than you, but I damn sure know when you done got a hold of some good pipe," Big Mama said, and Tiff looked down at her food like that bitch was gone walk off her plate. Big Ma, Cas, and Zoe burst out laughing, and I was looking from they ass to Tiff. It took a minute for me to realize what the fuck went down.

"My fuckin' nigga!" This nigga was about to shake some shit up and act a fuckin' fool. Tiff better be ready 'cause she done fucked up and let that nigga in.

Chapter Eight
CANNON

I can't believe I fucked up like that. I had no intentions on fucking with Tiff ever the fuck again. Don't get it twisted I'm still pissed the fuck off with her ass. Having her in my house and being that close to her just pulled that shit out of me. The need to punish her pussy was too much for a nigga like me to handle. Now that I've been inside and feeling the way her pussy gripped my dick, it's a fuckin' problem for me. It was almost seven in the evening, and I haven't heard shit from Shawn with my damn car. I can't believe I let that nigga drive my Rolls Royce Wraith. Grabbing my phone, I dialed his ass up.

"Yeah."

"Bruh, where is my damn car?" The nigga sounded like he was sleep.

"My bad, I had a long night and morning. I'm about to get up and I'll drop it off," he spoke.

"Just meet me at Ma house. She's been calling me like crazy, and we were supposed to stop by the other day. You still got shorty with you?" I asked him.

"Yeah, she gone chill here until I get back."

"Damn! You never let a chick stay over. Britt must have given you some special pussy," I laughed.

"Nigga! All I can do is throw up my hands, saying thank you to the man and say hallelujah," he burst out laughing.

"Boy, you stupid! Ok, Neyo, I'll be there in twenty minutes," I told him, hanging up and ordering me an Uber. It took me a few minutes for the Uber to come, and by the time I got to my mom's, Shawn was pulling up.

"Right on time, 'cause I damn sure was gone wait in the car for yo' ass. I wasn't about to get cussed out by myself. We in this shit together, nigga." We both burst out laughing because I felt the same damn way. We gone take this abuse together. Our mama didn't play with us at all with her crazy ass. Using my key to get inside the house, we could hear her talking shit on the phone with her best friend, Sherry. We walked into the kitchen and she damn near drop the phone.

"Sherry, let me call you back in a minute. My two knuckle-head ass boys done walked they ass up in here like they right," she spoke, and I knew she was gone be on one.

"Ma, before you even start, we got caught up handling business." Shawn knew damn well she didn't give a damn about what we had going on.

"Nigga, shut yo' dumb ass up and sit down. I swear to God y'all gone make me sucker slide y'all asses! I have been calling both of you, and y'all asses don't answer your damn phones. It could be an emergency, and y'all wouldn't know shit. I know this; you better get your shit together and act like you got some damn sense. Cedes been talking about moving out, and I need y'all to talk to her. She done got with that no-good ass nigga, and I know he's the reason she wants to go. He's always yelling at Jeremiah and I'm not having that. She damn sure won't be taking Jeremiah with her, y'all better talk to her." She talking to us like we can make Cedes stay.

"Ma, Mercedes is grown. If she wants to move out, then you can't stop her from doing that, but if a nigga mistreating Jeremiah, now that's a different conversation. You're gonna have to let go at some point and live your life for a change. Stop worrying about us and stop stressing yourself over something that eventually has to happen." I needed her to really think about what I was saying to her. I'm going to have a talk with my sister, and if I find out that nigga she's messing with is fuckin' with my nephew, then we got a problem.

"Bryshere, I'm not trying to hear that y'all grown shit. Besides, this house is too big for me to be in here by myself. If she moves out, I'm gone sell it and move in with you or your brother." I felt that shit in my dick 'cause if she moved in with me, my boy wouldn't get no action. Lil' mama can't move in with me, hell nawl!

"What! Nahh, dukes, get that out your thought process. I like to watch my girl ass bounce when she walks, and I can't do that shit if yo' cock blocking ass in the next room. You will straight fuck up my vibe. Bry, will buy you a smaller crib!" Shawn dumb ass said, and she popped his ass upside his head. Only my family called me by my legal name.

"Ma, we will talk to her about it, but for now, you need to focus on you," I said to her kissing her cheek.

"Ok, I will leave it alone and let you handle it. What's this I hear about Tiffany being home and got a baby? Now that's some shit right there. I hope you don't get all worked up over it. If she's not bothering you, just let her be, and hopefully, you won't have to cross paths with her," she stated.

"Too late, paths have been crossed, and this nigga done showed his entire ass." I wanted to punch this nigga in his throat

"Bryshere Mason! Please tell me you didn't hurt that girl." She looked at me with concern in her eyes. When I was going through my shit, my mom was the only one that could keep me together. I was ready to kill Tiff and it took a lot to get my shit together.

"She good, we had a talk, and that's it." I shrugged.

"Yo, I need to get back to the house, baby girl hungry. Ma, I will check on you in a couple of days to make sure you straight." I'm glad Shawn interrupted because this is a conversation I didn't want to have.

"I love you, ma." I pulled her in for a hug and we headed for the door.

"Bro, you better find Brenda a new house or talk Mercedes into staying home. 'Cause I'm telling you now, I can't do it. I love my mama to death and will lay a nigga down over her, but we can't live under the same roof. She would fuck up my pussy rotation, my dick already feeling some type of way just having this damn conversation." This nigga was crazy.

"Nigga, if we have to buy her something smaller, best believe you coming up off that bread," I laughed at his ass. Thirty minutes later, I was pulling in front of his crib. We dapped it up and he jumped out. I decided to stop by one of my traps to make sure things were good.

"Yo, where Brock at?" I asked, walking inside.

"He's in the back doing the count," Lonnie spoke as he continued to bag up our product.

"Sup? How is business treating us?" I questioned, walking into the room and taking a seat.

"We good over here. I meant to call you earlier. I saw your girl at the mall with her dude. Why you ain't tell me she was back in town? She said she was getting married out in Cali later this year." The more people bring her up, the more pissed I get. My phone was going off. Dena calling. I guess she was over being mad at me, and now her ass wanted to get dicked down.

"Yeah."

"So, you wasn't going to call me and apologize?" I can't believe she was really trying to keep this shit going.

"D, I apologized to you, shorty the day it happened. Why are you calling me on some bullshit? You know I don't do that back and forth shit." All she wanted to do was argue, and that shit was irritating as fuck to me.

"I want to see you. I miss you baby and I just got upset. You know I be in my feelings when it comes to that bitch." I swear this girl be giving me crazy vibes when dealing with her ass. She gone make me choke the shit out of her with the name calling shit.

"Yo, watch your fuckin' mouth, and I'm not in the mood to chill tonight. I will call you when I need some pussy." I hung up on her ass.

"Man, take your angry energy ass on up out of here. We got good vibes going on and I don't need that shit around me. I don't want that shit rubbing off on me. I need to get me some pussy and if I go home with an attitude, I can kiss the pussy goodbye! So, bye, nigga!" I had to laugh at this crazy nigga. Brock and I have been rocking since grade school. His mom is Ms. Sherry, my mom best friend.

"Fuck you, nigga! I hope Asia stops all pussy action on yo' ass," I burst out laughing 'cause this nigga face was priceless.

"Hatin ass nigga!" He yelled as I walked out to head home. By the time I got home, it was a little after eleven. Walking into my bedroom, I could still smell her scent, and my dick instantly got hard. Just thinking about her ass being laid up next to that nigga was pissing me off. I've never wanted anything in my life as bad as I wanted her ass right now, and I get what I want. I snatched up my keys and left out; it took me about twenty minutes to get over to her mother's house. Parking across the street, I sent her a text.

Me: *Come sit on my dick.*

Tiff: *What? I can't do that. You know my fiancé is here, Cannon.*

Me: *I'm outside, don't make me show my ass!*

She didn't text back, so I assumed she was coming out. A few minutes later, she was walking her beautiful ass out the door. I guess having a baby enhanced her weight because damn, this girl was fine as fuck. The way her hips swayed back and forth as she walked, always had my ass drooling.

"Cannon, are you crazy? This is fucked up on so many levels. Are you trying to cause problems for me? Look, I enjoyed every minute of being with you last night. I just can't do that shit; I'm engaged to be married," she sighed with her face twisted.

"That sounds like a YOU problem. Just as long as that nigga don't put his hands on you. I don't give a fuck about this lil' bullshit ass relationship. So, when you stopped fuckin' with me, you decided you didn't want to fuck with women anymore?" I asked her. We had an agreement that if she ever got the urge to be with a woman, she would let me know.

"I've changed, you know that shit happens right. Just because I've been with women don't mean I can't go back to fucking men," she snapped.

"I'm just curious as to how you got with this sucker ass dude. But fuck all that. I need some pussy, and the only pussy I want to feel is yours. So, I needed you to come ride this dick," I told her as I unzipped my pants and freed my lil' homie.

"Nigga, you crazy as hell. I'm not gone fuck you while my dude is inside the house." Reaching over, I pushed her legs apart and rubbed my fingers on her fat ass pussy through the fabric of her shorts.

"Ahhhhhh!" A moan escaped her beautiful ass lips, and I knew I had her. I slid my fingers inside of her shorts, massaging her clit. The more I rubbed her shit, the louder she became as she gyrated her pussy on my fingers.

"You gave that nigga some pussy?" I asked her because if she did, I was gone kill his ass. I don't know how she was gone work that shit out. All I know is that nigga better not ever smell or taste this pussy again.

"No," she groaned as I tugged at her shorts to pull them off.

"Come get on this dick, baby." Pulling her over into my lap, hovering over me, I slid my dick back and forth over her slit.

"Cannon, this is so... Arghhhh! Wrong," she whispered as I guided her down on my dick.

"Fuck! This pussy is good as fuck," I gritted, gripping her ass while she moved up and down.

"Ohhhh, this dick feels fuckin' good," she whispered, biting down on her bottom lip. The fuck faces that she was making was killing a nigga. Coming over here was a bad idea because this the type of pussy that will have you on a murder spree. As I fucked the shit out of her, all I could think about is different ways to kill her nigga.

"That's it, baby. Ride the fuck out of this dick!" I growled, pounding her shit out.

"Cannonnn! Damn, I miss this dick. I lov..." She was so caught up that she slipped up.

"Say that shit, baby! Say what the fuck you feel!" I roared, fucking that shit out of her.

"I...I love you! Ohh God! I'm cumming!" She screamed, and those words sent me over the edge.

"Gotdamn!" Cum shot through my ass so hard I felt paralyzed. I couldn't move and she was still riding my dick trying to get her another nut. Gathering my composure, I lifted her off me and pulled her out of the car. Picking her up, pinning her against the car as she eased down on my dick, I was so hungry for this girl I wanted her to feel this dick. Slamming inside of her, she held onto my neck and cried out my name. Neither of us gave a fuck that we were outside of her mother's house with her so-called fiancé steps away. This was a dangerous game we were playing, and I didn't give a fuck as long as I had her wrapped around my dick.

The sound of my doorbell was going off and I had just slid out of the pussy. I don't know what the fuck lil' mama got inside her shit. That shit was causing my ass to have abandonment issues. I can't tell you how many times I done fucked her ass in almost forty-eight hours.

"Fuck! Who the fuck is ringing my damn doorbell like that?" I barked, throwing on my sweats. Snatching my door open, I wanted to dropkick this hoe back to where she came from.

"Hey, can we talk for a minute?" I couldn't believe Stacia was standing at my fuckin' door.

"Nah, now isn't a good time. I have company, and it's disrespectful as fuck to be standing here talking to you. You know what it is, there are no second chances with me. You wanted to fuck the homie, and you lucky I didn't slice your fuckin' throat behind it," I told her.

Stacia and I had been together for a year when she decided that she wanted to hop on the next nigga dick. There is one thing that I'm big on, and that's loyalty. If a bitch can't be loyal to me, then I don't want her. I was really feeling her ass, and then she goes and do some dumb shit like that.

"Babe, are you coming back to bed?" I heard from behind me, and a smile formed on my face. When I turned to respond to Brittany, my dick instantly got hard because her ass was standing there, butt ass naked. Baby girl was thick as hell, but she didn't have an overly big ass. Her deep brown eyes and medium brown complexion complimented her, and she was fine as fuck, just the way I liked my woman. I guess the shit she was doing was my payback for answering her phone. Stacia looked as if she wanted to spit fire on both of our asses. I just slammed and locked the door, walking up on Britt, pulling her back to bed.

"Yo, I see you on some petty shit," I spoke, kissing her on her lips.

"Nah, I was just ready for you to come back to bed. But seriously, I think it's time for you to take me to Tiff's mama house. I don't want to fuck up nothing you got going on," she said, and I wasn't feeling her leaving right now.

"Baby girl, you not fucking a damn thing up over here. If I had a woman, you wouldn't have your fine ass in here. I'm a grown ass man; I don't cheat on my woman because I know better. I don't play with people's feelings 'cause that shit will get you killed. When I make a move and make you my girl, it's gone be you that fucked up. Which is why that bitch is on the other side of the door. Don't ask me a question you really don't want the answer to, because I'm gone give you the truth. I will never lead a female on. If this is just a fuck for me, I'm gone let you know what it is. Now come lay your fine ass down and let me suck that pussy to sleep," I told her. She climbed in bed and I did just what I said I would do.

The next morning, I heard loud talking and jumped out of bed, grabbing my gun. The closer I got to the noise, all I could do was brace my damn self. Walking into the kitchen Brittany was standing at the stove with one of my shirts on, and I could see most of her naked ass.

"Ma, what the hell are you doing over here?" I asked.

"I wanted to come over and cook you some breakfast, but I see you got your flavor of the night here. Baby, you will get more respect if you date him before giving up the ass. Let this nigga wine and dine you for a little while. Stop hopping on the dick 'cause the nigga look good on the outside. Just because they look good to you doesn't mean they good for you. This nigga could be batshit crazy, and you don't find out until after you done had his baby and said I do. I was gone call you a bunch of hoes, but my spirit is feeling good today. So, I decided to drop a few gems on you. Shawn, I will talk to your hoe ass later, baby." She smiled, walking to the door.

"Bruh, you gone make me take my key," I said, shaking my head at her rude ass.

"Boy, go to hell, you ain't taking shit. I'm about to go

check on your brother and see what his crazy ass up to, and your ass better not tell him I'm coming over." When she walked out, I slammed the door.

"Yo, I'm sorry, baby girl. My mom can be rude as fuck sometimes." I hope what my dukes said didn't offend her.

"I don't bend easily, and for some reason, what she said was right. Now how she said it was a little out of line, but I get it. We're good. I'm about to go get dressed so you can drop me off." She left the kitchen and I followed behind her.

"I'm going to drop you off so you can check in with your people. I'm coming back to get you after I handle some business. Maybe we can go get some dinner later if you good with that."

For some reason, I didn't want her to feel like she was just a fuck to me. Even though we just met, I was feeling her. I learned the insides of that pussy and can break that shit down like a fraction. If another nigga goes inside her, other than me, my ass gone know about it. Besides that, we had some meaningful conversations. I got to know her, and she definitely got to know a little about me.

Chapter Ten

TIFF

This shit is getting out of hand, and I'm fucking up big time. I can't believe I fell weak to this man. I didn't think that he would want anything to do with me, and all of a sudden, he's pounding my insides oh so fuckin' good. I've cheated on my man, and all I could think about was when I would get my next hit of Cannon. The thought of him massaging my insides was driving my ass crazy. I called Brittany and told her to get her ass here now.

"Tiffany, what is going on with you? I thought you said you were staying, and he was leaving today?" My mom asked when I walked into her bedroom to pack up Aniya's clothes.

"Ma, it's just best that I go back. I promise I will be back to visit you as soon as I can. Things are getting out of hand and I can't be here right now." I know she's upset that we're leaving, but It's for the best.

"The only thing that's getting out of hand is that you're about to make the biggest mistake of your life and marry a man that you don't even love. The man you love and want is the man that had you screaming to the Good lawd above when you took your hot ass outside and took a ride on the stairway to heaven with his ass." She smirked, and my damn mouth dropped to the floor.

"Oh my God! You saw us? What if Marlo saw us?" I was pacing back and forth, nervous as hell.

"Girl, that nigga was asleep. I was watching your back anyway. I would have sent a fire signal to your ass if he had woken up. I just need you to think about all of this shit. I think you're settling for something that you don't have to settle for. You can have the real deal if you just go to him. I know you're thinking about Aniya. You have to do what makes you happy, baby, and something tells me it's much more to that nigga than you know. I've always been able to tell when a nigga full of shit and that nigga you got in there got shit running out his ass." I heard what she was saying. I just didn't want my daughter growing up with her parents in separate homes.

"Mom, I will be alright." I was so embarrassed to know that she knew what I did last night. When I got the text from Cannon, Marlo had already fallen asleep. After I came back in and washed up, I felt like shit for betraying him. So, I decided this morning to go back to Cali with him. If I wanted shit to work with us, I had to leave here and be dedicated to my fiancé.

"You got all your things packed?" Marlo questioned as he grabbed his bags.

"Yeah, we have to wait on Britt. She should be here in a few. I purchased her ticket last night when I got mine," I told him.

"Man, fuck her. She should've had her ass here and stop being a hoe! That's why I told you to stop hanging with her ass. She was happy as hell that nigga took you and I don't want that bitch in my house. It's either going to be me and your daughter or her, and that's all I'm going to say about that." I get that he's angry, but threatening me about my child will get his ass fucked up.

"I'm not getting into this shit with you. Just know we gone have problems when you involve my daughter. As for Brittany, she does what the fuck she wants. I can't tell her how to live her life. Nor can you tell me that I can't hang with my best friend. We've been through this and ain't shit changed!" I walked out of the room, bumping into Britt.

"That nigga still on his bitch shit about me, but as always, fuck him!" She spoke.

"Britt, where the hell have you been?" I asked, smiling at her.

"Having the time of my fuckin' life. Just thinking about his ass gives me the shakes. Soooo, did you get dicked down by a real nigga, or you still getting poked by a pencil dick nigga?" She burst out laughing and I pulled her down the hall into the kitchen.

"Sis, that nigga fucked me so good I can still feel him

inside of me, and I can barely move. When I walk, my pussy is screaming, which is why we're getting the fuck out of here. I got you a ticket, and you need to go pack your shit; we leave to go back to Cali in a few hours." The look on her face let me know that she wasn't feeling it.

"What! I'm not trying to leave right now. I have plans on getting with Shawn tonight. What happened to us staying for a week?" She questioned with her face frowned up.

"Britt, I'm losing control being back home near him. I fucked Cannon out front last night with Marlo in here sleeping. Now you know that's some disrespectful shit. I'm afraid of what he's doing to me and the way I'm feeling," I sighed.

"Yes, the fuck you can. I would be riding that dick so good Marlo bitch ass would feel it in his muthafuckin' sleep!" We both burst out laughing because this girl was nuts.

"Britt, please do this for me. We can come back when I get stronger. I need to be far away from him, I had no idea that he would forgive me."

"Wheew weeee, this nigga Cannon got that disrespectful dick. He done made a bitch wanna run or throw it all away. I know that's the fuck right! Biihhhhh, you sound like yo' ass just had major surgery or some shit. Ummm, who forgave you though, sis? I don't think you're forgiven just yet. He fuckin' his way to that point. Right now, yo' ass is getting revenge fucked, and I know that pipe down is something serious! Let me go pack my damn bag and call Shawn. You owe me for this shit. I'm changing my seat on the plane, I don't want to be nowhere near fuck nigga row." Shaking my head as she walked out, I headed to the room to go pack.

---

*I*t was going on five West Coast time by the time we got home. I was exhausted from traveling, and all I wanted to do was sleep. I decided to take a nice warm shower so that I could climb in bed. Closing my eyes as the water cascaded down my body caused my mind to drift back to the night in Cannon's bed. That man had a way of making me feel like I was going to combust inside. Just his touch did something to me. It was nothing and no one that could make me feel the way he did. It's just when shit went bad with us, I thought there was no hope for us. The thoughts of him and me rubbing the soap on my body made me hot, and my pussy was throbbing. Sliding my fingers between my thighs, rubbing my clit had me feeling so good that I needed to cum. Grinding against my fingers with thoughts of him pounding my insides relentlessly.

"Sssss, fuck!" The sensation felt so good I couldn't stop the moans that escaped my mouth.

"Let me help you with that," Marlo whispered as he began massaging my clit and moving my hand out the way. I was so horny, but I know I shouldn't be sleeping with him right now.

"Babe, I just want to cum quick! I...I don't Ahhhhhhhhh," I cried out as he pushed himself inside, pounding me like he had something to prove and wasn't proving shit. I was damn turned off; my pussy got dry.

"Fuck! You been denying me this pussy for days now! Fuck! This pussy good. Throw that shit back," he growled, and I couldn't do it. It was like everything went cold and I no longer wanted to cum. The messed-up thing is I feel like I'm cheating on Cannon. What the fuck is going on with me?

"You feel that shit?! Cum with me, babe 'cause I'm about to bust," he gritted as he released, and I faked as if I was cumming with him. After I got out the shower and got in bed, Marlo came out of his closet fully dressed and grabbing his keys off the dresser.

"I need to go check on my spots and make sure everything good. I shouldn't be long."

I didn't care that he was leaving; this wasn't nothing new. His ass is always gone, and it was always to handle his business. Just as soon as I got into a deep sleep, I heard my phone vibrating. Picking it up and noticing that it was a text message.

Unknown: *So, you leave and don't say shit to me about it?!*

Me: *Cannon, we had to come back home. I didn't think that I had to say anything to you. What we did was a mistake, I'm getting married, and I can't be involved with you. I wish things could have been different, but I can't do this to a man that loves me unconditionally. He's my daughters' father. I have to think about her in all of this.*

Unknown: *Bet! Live yo' life, beautiful.*

Me: *Thank you, I'm glad you understand.*

He never responded, and I know he was pissed off. I don't

know what the fuck is wrong with me. I'm as tough as they come, but when it comes to him, I act all soft and shit. I assumed he found out that I left from his brother or Nas. I did call them and let them know I was leaving to come back home. I had a talk with Nasir and Priest about being at my wedding. I would like for my family to be here, and they agreed to put shit aside and come out for the wedding, which was five months away. I erased all of the text messages between Cannon and I and drifted into a good sleep.

Chapter Eleven

BRITTANY

*T*hree months Later

Shawn and I have been talking every day, and I even snuck my lil' thot hot box ass back to Philadelphia to see him for a week. The connection we've made with each other is crazy, and I'm feeling him something serious. Even though we're just getting to know each other, he keeps saying that I won't be living in Cali much longer. I'm not just ready to give up all that I have going on here and move back to Philly with a man I'm just getting to know. Tiff and I own a clothing boutique here in LA, and our business is booming right now. We're planning on opening a second store soon. So, moving isn't the best option for me, and I kind of hinted at that, but he ignored the topic. I heard my phone going off and I ran to go grab it.

"Hey, boo. What's up?" I asked Tiff.

"Hey, do you still have those nausea pills that the doctor gave you a while back?" She questioned.

"Uhhh, I think I have a few left, let me go check. Why, what's wrong?"

"I feel sick, I can't stop throwing up, and this shit is irritating the fuck out of me. I can't go to the doctor's until tomorrow. I just can't go through this shit all night long." I felt bad for her because she sounded horrible.

"Yeah, I got some. You coming to get them, or do you need me to bring them over?" I knew she probably didn't feel like driving.

"No, Marlo is on your side of town, and I will have him stop by and get them," she spoke.

"Alright, I will have them waiting for him. Ohhhh, shit! Do you think you're pregnant again? Remember you were like this when you were pregnant with Aniya! Bihhhhhhhhhh!!!! When you were bustin' it open for a real nigga did you use protection? Lawdddd please say you did 'cause babbbbyyyy, this shit bout to get realer than a muthafucka, and I think I want to rent me a place across the street from you. I can't miss none of this muthafuckin' hot ass tea!" I was sitting on pins and needles waiting for her ass to answer the damn question.

"Ummm, no. We were in the heat of the moment; none of that was on our minds. Ohhh my God! I've slept with Marlo several times since him. I can't be pregnant; this can't happen to me! Fuck!" She panicked.

"Babbbbby, oh my God is right! You better gone and call

on him 'cause yo' ass is gone need all the power He possesses to calm the storm that's coming your way. But I'm here for you, sis. You need me to go to the doctors with you?" I asked her because I wanted to witness all this good fuckery.

"Britt, this shit is not funny! I may have royally fucked up," she yelled.

"Nahh, boo, ain't no maybe in this shit right here. You got into an entanglement, and now yo' ass is tangled the fuck up round this bitch," I laughed and her ass hung up on me. Poor Lil Tink she done danced with the devil and now gotta call on the power of Jesus to get her ass out of this mess. Just as I went to grab my Chicken bowl from Chipotle out of the fridge, my doorbell was going off. Peeping through the peep-hole, I saw that it was Marlo punk ass coming to pick up the medicine for Tiff. Opening the door, he tried walking in, and I stopped his ass.

"Nah, bruh, you can stand right here until I go grab them." Being around that fake ass nigga made my ass itch. Grabbing the pills and walking back out front, this nigga had done walked inside my shit and sitting on my couch.

"Nigga, didn't I tell your ass to wait outside?" I frowned.

"The fuck I look like standing outside for! What you got going on, trying to find the next nigga dick to hop on? I got a big nigga you can come see about whenever you ready." He smiled, grabbing his dick through his jeans.

"Nigga, I would never fuck with a pussy ass bitch like you. You foul as fuck for that shit, knowing me and Tiff rock hard. I should bust you in your muthafuckin' head for saying that shit. Get the fuck out of my shit!" I threw the bottle at his ass.

"Whatever, hoe! You better keep that shit to yourself, because she would never believe your hoe ass anyway." He headed for the door and left. I was so fuckin' mad I was shaking. I couldn't believe this punk ass bitch said that shit. Yeah, Tiff, gone have to hear about this shit. I wouldn't be a friend if I didn't tell her. Picking up my ringing phone, I was not paying attention to who was calling because I was so pissed.

"What!" I spoke.

"So, you finally answer your fuckin' phone and then pick up with an attitude? The fuck is wrong with you, Britt! You got a nigga answering your phone while y'all fuckin'?! I thought we were supposed to be working our shit out."

This nigga was beyond mad. I had been avoiding his calls, not answering my door and for the last few months. I was being a lil' punk 'cause I didn't want to argue with him about me not wanting to be with him. He was the one that fucked shit up with us. He was out fucking every bitch he could find, and he was the one that got caught the hell up. I guess I did lead him to believe that as long as he was trying, we could work on getting back together.

I have been with Tre for five years, and to find out he was doing me like that was heartbreaking. It took me a long ass time to get my shit together over this nigga. So, when Shawn answered my phone, that shit made me smile on the inside to know that he was feeling how I did when he hurt me.

"Look, I know what we were trying to do, and I know that

shit was a little messed up. But maybe I need to just take some time to rethink everything," I told him.

"Are you serious? You really doing this shit right now? After all of the progress I've made to show you that I'm all about you! As soon as I come back in town, we gone sit down and talk about this shit, Britt. I fuckin' love you and I'm not going to allow you to just say fuck us." He hung up, and I had to look at my damn phone. I guess his ass ain't giving up that easy. Urggghhhhh! I hate being in difficult shit. This night turned into some depressing shit, so I called it a night.

———

*M*y phone jolted me out of my sleep, and I was tired as fuck. I let that shit go to voicemail and it started back up again. Snatching it off of my night-stand, I saw that it was Tiff calling.

"Hey, sis," I groggily spoke.

"Britt, where are you! I thought you were meeting me at the doctor's office," she sighed.

"Oh shit! What time is it?"

"You got thirty minutes; I have been calling you for the past hour. Urggghhh, hurry up, Britt!" She hung up on my ass. Jumping out of bed, I rushed to take a shower and left out because LA traffic is a bitch. By the time I got to her doctor's office, they had already called her back, and the nurse took me back to her.

"Damn, I'm so glad you made it. They already took a urine

sample from me, and I'm just waiting for the doctor to come in," she said, throwing her hand over her face.

"Bruh, I wish we could smoke when we get out of here, but something tells me that shit won't be happening today." I smiled, and I know she wished she would have left my ass where I was. A few minutes later, the doctor walked into the room.

"Hello, Ms. Bryant. I understand that you're nauseated and having some back and stomach pain?" He questioned her.

"Yes, it's been going on for a few days now, and it just got worse yesterday," she told him.

"We did a pregnancy test on you. The results were positive, so that's the reason you're nauseated and having the discomfort in your stomach and back. I'm going to check you out, we can tell you how far along you are and try to get you feeling better," he spoke, and Tiff ass almost fell off the table.

"Oh my God, I get a hold of some monster dick and lose my mind being careless and shit! Dr. Barringer, are you sure? Can you take the test again?" She asked him. It was the monster dick and the look on the doctor's face, for me. My good sis was losing her shit behind this tea the good ole doc was giving.

"Ms. Bryant, the test results are accurate. There is no need to retake it. You're definitely pregnant, lay back, and let me get your exam done." He walked to the door and called the nurse into the room. An hour later, we were walking out with Tiff in a panic and almost eleven weeks pregnant.

"Britt, I have no idea what I'm going to do. I'm so glad

that Marlo went out of town this morning and couldn't come with me. I have to make some shit up. There is no way I can tell him right now," she cried.

"Tiff, I don't think Marlo is the person that you truly need to be worried about. If Cannon ever finds out that you're pregnant, knowing it's a possibility that could be his baby, your problems with Marlo is going to be minimal compared to the shit you're going to have with him. And how the hell do you expect to hide the shit when you're three months pregnant? Let's go have lunch. Maybe it will ease your mind. Where is Aniya if Marlo's out of town?" I asked her as we walked to our cars.

"She's with his mom for a couple of days since I wasn't feeling well. I'm so glad she does have her because I need this time to think." She shrugged. I felt bad for her, but the shit was still hilarious.

"I need to talk to you about something, but I will tell you after you calm down a little." I was going to talk to her about what happened with Marlo, but decided to tell her later she has a lot on her mind.

"You can tell me now; it can't be worse than this shit. I'm going to ride with you, and we can come back for my car later. Let's go to Shaquille's since we're close by," she spoke as she got inside of my car.

"Nah, we can wait until later," I stated. Once we made it to the restaurant, we had to wait until our name was called.

"I sure hope the wait isn't lo..." Something grabbed her

attention, and I turned to see what the hell she was looking at.

"Is that Marlo?" I questioned just as she took off walking. Marlo bitch ass was sitting at a table having lunch with this chick, and she was holding a baby.

"Who the fuck is this?!" She yelled, walking up on them.

"Fuck! Tiff, ummmm..." This nigga couldn't even get his words together.

"Who the fuck are you, walking up on us asking damn questions?!" The girl put her baby down and jumped up in Tiff's face.

"Bitch, it's best if you sit the fuck down. This shit ain't about you, and I promise I don't want to beat yo' ass over this nigga. Marlo, who the fuck is she?" Tiff asked, resting her hand on her waist.

"I'm the mother of his child and his fiancé." And when this bitch flashed her ring in Tiff's face, I almost flatlined. Her damn ring was the exact ring on Tiff's finger, and the baby couldn't have been no more than six or seven months old. So, this hoe and Tiff were pregnant around the same time.

"What! So, how the fuck you thought this was gone work! Is that your baby, Marlo?!" Tiff screamed, and I knew my girl was about to explode on his ass.

"Yeah, but let's talk about this shit outside, you in here causing a scene and shit," This pussy ass nigga spoke.

"Nigga, fuck you! You out here got me looking like a fool. How long have you been with him?" Tiff asked the chick.

"None of your fucking business!" She spat, and I swear I was ready to tag this hoe.

"Nigga, you ain't shit! Tiff, this is what I wanted to talk to you about. When this pussy came over to my house last night, he was trying to get me to fuck him. I kicked his ass out of my shit; you were so upset I didn't want to tell you. But after seeing this shit, you need to get rid of this goofy ass nigga!" I told her, and the tears started to flow. I knew when that happened, she was going to fuck this nigga up. Maybe I should have waited.

"You tried to fuck with my best friend!" She yelled.

"Tiff, this bitch lying!" Marlo grabbed her arm and tried pulling her towards the door.

"You not about to go talk to her. Why the fuck she so mad over you being with me, nigga?" The chick questioned.

"Excuse me. I'm going to have to ask all of you to leave," the manager stated when he approached us.

"Char, chill the fuck out and take my son home," Marlo gritted on her and she didn't move. Before he could react, Tiff was throwing blows all on that nigga head. He must have forgotten who the fuck he was fucking with. Tiff had done a three-sixty with her attitude, but don't get it twisted; she will fuck yo ass up.

"Bitch, get the fuck off my man!" This Char chick yelled, as she tried to swing on Tiff, and that was a bad decision on her part because I beat that bitch ass. The next thing I knew, we were being pulled apart and handcuffed. The manager had called the police on us, and I was even more pissed because they only took me and Tiff to jail.

Chapter Twelve

NAS

I was on my way to meet up with the guys. Pop & Stepmama just got back in town, and he wanted to catch up on what's been going on. As I pulled into the parking lot, Cannon pulled in behind me.

"What's up?" I spoke.

"Chillin." He shrugged as we walked into Brenda's. I had to sit down and really have a talk with this nigga. I don't know what my cousin did to his ass, but this nigga was geeking the fuck out.

"What up, old man? I feel like I haven't seen your ass in years. Stepmama done finally let yo' ass up for air," I laughed.

"Man, I'm loving every bit of my beautiful wife. She can suffocate me, and it wouldn't bother me one bit." He smiled, sipping on his drink.

"Nah, a nigga gotta breathe. I love my bear, but she not

about to be taking my muthafuckin' air. Fuck around, and I would be looking and acting like this lunatic ass nigga," I burst out laughing, looking over at Cannon's ass.

"Man, fuck you," he chuckled.

"Cannon, what's up with you, man? I heard Tiff came home a few months ago and caused you to lose your mind," Pop said to him.

"Where did you hear that from?" He questioned.

"Big Mama said you beat her man's ass, took his woman, dog walked her on the devil's dick, and then gave her back with a new lease on life." We all burst out laughing because Big Mama was a damn fool.

"I'm good, shorty doing her and we both moving on. Dena and I are in a relationship now, and life is good." Cannon shrugged.

"When that happened?" I asked him.

"We made shit official last night." I couldn't believe this nigga got with Dena money hungry ass. He and I both knew she wasn't the perfect match for him. I was all for him getting him a woman, but Dena just wasn't it.

"Bro, if you're still feeling some type of way about this situation, you not over her. I wouldn't give up on her, if that's what you want. Tiff feels like she would be letting her daughter down, and to be honest, I think that's the only reason she would give up her happiness. I've talked to her, and that's what I took from the conversation. She's not in a good headspace, and I think that has something to do with you," Priest said to him, and he just sat there sipping on his drink.

"Yeah, well, she made her decision. I'm not chasing no woman that's not even in the game to be chased," he stated.

"I'm with Priest. If you love her, I wouldn't give up so easy. Pray on it and ask God to give you some guidance," Pop told him.

"Pop! This nigga done murdered hundreds of niggas just 'cause they ass was trying to breathe the same air as him. The only guidance God gone give his ass is the directions to hell." They were laughing, but I was serious.

"I know she's your family and I don't want to be disrespectful. In my mind, shit between us is over, and there is no need to go back and forth about it. Let's talk business. The operation is growing, and we've generated more money than we've ever seen. There is another business that I think we should look into, and it's just as lucrative as the drug game. I have a connect for guns. He can get us whatever we want when we want them," Cannon spoke.

"I'm not sure how I feel about flooding the streets with guns." I almost broke my damn neck to look at my brother.

"Nigga, you flood them with drugs, so what the fuck is the difference?!" I questioned.

"I flood the streets with my diamonds and collect my money from y'all illegal ass niggas." He smiled.

"Whatever helps you sleep at night. Hey, Casey. I need you to put me an order in," I told her.

"Sure, what can I get you?" She smiled.

"Let me get a bacon cheeseburger with everything on it,

ten hot wings, and some cheese fries. Ohhh, and let me get some of those crab balls."

"You sure you ordered enough?" Cannon looked at me.

"All I know is y'all better order 'cause you damn sure ain't getting none of my shit." They put their orders in because they asses knew I wasn't playing.

"What's up, Cannon?" Diamond funky ass spoke, walking up to us.

"Bitch!" He snapped, looking her up and down.

"How have you been?" She asked him, and I had to step in before this nigga made the wrong move.

"He got married today at 11:13. He don't fuck with funky ass hoes no mo, and he ain't never gone forget how your hoe ass slipped on another nigga dick in his crib. I heard your new nigga came up missing. How that shit been working out for you? You may need to keep your ass away from this nigga 'cause he not stable, and the death rate can go up by one hoe in the next two minutes," I told her. This nigga pulled his gun out, looking at it, rubbing it, and then pointed it at her. While Priest ass was about to bust a lung from laughing so damn hard. The chick Diamond was with was damn near dragging her ass out the door.

"Boy, yo' ass is crazy!" Pop shook his head.

"She lucky I was there to save her ass. Had this nigga been alone, he might have put a slug or two in her." They know I was telling the truth. I got a call from an unknown number, I ignored the call and they called right back.

"Yeah."

"Hello, I'm trying to reach Nas. My name is Kelly and I work for Tiffany."

"What's up? Why are you calling me and not Tiff?" I asked her.

"She asked me to call you; she's been arrested and can't get to her money. She said you will send me the money to bail her and Brittany out. If you can, please send me the money. She's pregnant, and I really need your help getting them out of there." This girl was talking so damn fast. I heard two things that were of importance: jail and pregnant.

"Jail! Pregnant! What the fuck is she doing in jail?" I blurted out, and all eyes were on me.

"It's a long story, but I'm sure she will explain it when she talks to you." I know Tiff didn't get her ass locked up, and she got a damn baby.

"Text me the best way to send this money to you and how much you need. I'm on my way to LA. Can you send me her address and where she's being held? Hopefully, you will have her out by the time I get there." I finished talking to her and ended the call.

"Everything good?" Priest looked over at me.

"Nah, we need to go. Can you call and get us a plane headed to LA? I will meet you at the airport in an hour." I didn't have to explain shit, we stood, and everyone followed me out of the restaurant.

"Do you need me on this?" Pop questioned.

"Nah, we're good. I will call you when we land." I dapped him up and he walked back inside.

"What's up, bro?" Cannon waited for me to start talking.

"Tiff and Brittany are both in jail. I'm not sure what the fuck they did, but I have to go find out. You got your shit going with Dena, so I don't expect you to take this flight with us. If we need you, I will call you. I think Priest and I got it from here," I told him.

"Nah, I got the part about her being in jail, but I'm gone need you to elaborate on the pregnant part. Who's pregnant?" He asked, and I couldn't lie to my boy.

"The chick Kelly that called me said that she was in jail and pregnant. I'm not sure if she was talking about Tiff, or Britt. That's all I know. As soon as I find out what's going on, I will call you." I had a feeling that she was talking about Tiff. I knew this nigga would be on edge, so I kept my thoughts to myself.

"Don't take off without me and Shawn." I shook my head because shit in Cali was about to get real.

"I will text you the info as soon as I hear from Priest." I jumped in my car and called Cas to have her pack me a bag. Priest ass left as soon as we walked out of the restaurant. When it comes to family, we don't ask no questions. I know her bitch ass boyfriend better not have her doing no foul shit. I know he's in the streets, and if she got caught up on some shit he got going on, I'm gone kill that nigga.

Chapter Thirteen
CANNON

She thinks this shit a game! Tiff better pray that she's not the one pregnant. I called my brother, so that he could take this trip with us. I don't know the details of what he and Brittany have going on, but if she's the one pregnant, he needed to know about it. All I knew is that one of them was pregnant, and we gone get to the bottom of that shit asap. My phone was buzzing, and it was Shawn letting me know that he was pulling up. Hearing about the mess with Tiff caught me off guard that I forgot that Dena was coming over to spend the night with me.

"I can't believe this shit! We just made things official, and you're running off to go play captain save a hoe!" She yelled.

"I told you what was going on out of respect that you're my girl. I slept with her, you knew that, so don't act like this shit is a surprise to you. Now it's a possibility that she might be the one that's pregnant, and if that's the case, then I need to know if that's my kid. I will never be disrespectful to you; I just need to know what's going on. If you can't handle this part of it, let me know, and we can just end this shit before it gets started. I have to go. I will call you as soon as I get a chance." Dena and I had a conversation, and I told her every-thing about me and Tiff. I opened the door, and she walked out without saying goodbye. I got into the car with my brother.

"Sup." I dapped him up as he pulled out, jumping on the highway heading to the airport. I'm glad Priest rented a private plane; it was almost one in the morning by the time we made it to Cali.

"I just called Tiff and Britt's phone and didn't get an answer. I got a text from Kelly saying they were released around midnight. So, they should be home by now. Let's head over to Tiff's house," Nas stated.

"I'm with that shit," I spoke.

"I bet your angry ass is. Look, we gone go up in here on some calm shit until we find out what's going on with her." I just nodded because me staying calm will only happen depending on her response to the shit I needed to know. It took us about thirty minutes to get to her crib. When we got out, all we could hear was her yelling and shit crashing.

"What the fuck! If Tiff doesn't answer the door within a few minutes, then Cannon, you gone have to get us in," Nas spoke, pulling his gun out. Walking up to the front door, I kicked that muthafucka in fuck, waiting on somebody to come answer this bitch.

"Damn, nigga! Here you go with your shit, I said give her time to answer the muthafucka first."

"Man, fuck that!" I gritted as we walked inside.

"Who the fuck? Nigga, what the fuck you doing in my shit?" This bitch nigga came running down the steps.

"Yo, Tiff!" Priest called out for her.

"What are you guys doing here?" She asked, looking at her door.

"We got the call that you were locked the fuck up. What you thought we were gone be doing, twiddling our fuckin' thumbs? What the hell happened?" Nas asked her.

"This nigga is what happened. He got another bitch and baby that's only a few days younger than Ani..." She was cut off by bitch boy.

"These niggas don't need to know our business and they damn sure gonna have to get up out my shit! We on my turf now, muthafucka!" He barked, and Nas punched that nigga in his shit. He was swinging back but was no match for the blows Nas was giving. I know my boy had been itching to beat his ass. Priest and Shawn got shit under control and pulled Nas off him.

"Nigga, I've been trying to give yo' pussy ass a pass because of your daughter. Keep talking shit, and the only thing yo' bitch ass gone be spitting out is these fuckin' hollow tips. Tiff finish what the hell you were saying." Nas looked at her.

"I caught him with his bitch and son; we got into it, and a fight broke out. For some reason, Britt and I were the only ones arrested. I don't have anyone here other than Britt for family emergencies, and she was in jail with me. I called Kelly so that she could get in touch with you to get the money. She didn't say that y'all were coming out here," she spoke as she looked over at me.

"Are you pregnant?" I asked, stepping into her personal space.

"What! where did you hear that from?" She questioned with a shaky voice.

"Don't fuckin' play with me! Are you pregnant?!" I roared and she jumped.

"Pregnant! Why the fuck you asking if my girl pregnant? You need to get the fuck out of my damn house. You niggas not gone keep disrespecting me thinking shit sweet. I got something for yo' ass though, pussy!" He yelled, pulling out his gun, and I chuckled.

"Nigga, you must wanna die." Nas shook his head.

"You don't even get to talk shit when you got a whole baby out here and a bitch that's rockin' the same ring as me. Fuck you! This is my shit. Like I said before they came you need to get all your shit and get the fuck out!" She yelled at him while his gun was still pointed on me. No one made a move because they knew me and knew that I had it under control. I hate when a nigga pull his gun and don't use that shit.

"Man, fuck this bitch boy. Are you pregnant, and is that my fuckin' baby?" I asked her ass again, never breaking the stare I had on this nigga.

"Tiff, answer the damn question, so this nigga can show his ass.' Cause we all know what's getting ready to happen," Nas told her.

"Ye...Yes, I'm pregnant, and I don't know if you're the father." When this pussy realized what she was saying, he tried to charge at her but was halted when I sent my fist crashing into his face, knocking the gun out of his hand. He tried to go toe to toe with me, but my ass was out for blood and I tried to beat this nigga head in! When I said I was gone beat his ass every time I saw him, I meant that shit. I've never wanted to kill a man as bad as I wanted this nigga in the dirt.

"Where is your daughter?" Nas asked her, and that calmed me down a little because I really didn't want to show my ass with her kid in the house.

"She's upstairs. I went to pick her up from her grandmother's when I got out." She looked away, trying to avoid eye contact with me.

"This nigga gotta go, she doesn't want him here, and I'm tired of looking at his ass. Tiff, the next time you decided to get with a nigga make sure the dude can protect you at all cost. This nigga ain't nothing but talk. He done got his ass beat down twice within ten minutes, and he was the nigga with the gun," Priest told her and made the nigga get up and get the fuck out.

"Go get y'all shit! You're coming back to Philadelphia until you have the baby, and if you think for one second that you will do what you did to me again, there won't be nobody that's gone save your ass!" I said to her.

"I get that you're in your feelings. However, I have a business and a life here, and my daughters' family is here. I can't just up and leave like that, and you can't come up in here tossing out demands and shit. I have no plans on doing anything to harm my baby," she snapped.

"Get your shit! You have ten minutes, or I will start packing that shit for you. I don't give a damn about that pussy ass nigga, his family, or your attitude." She could come voluntary or I will drag her ass out of here involuntarily.

"Bro, let's go outside and get some fresh air." Shawn headed for the door and I walked out behind him. I was so fuckin' pissed that I put myself in this situation with her ass again. All I know is that she's bringing that ass back to Philadelphia. A few minutes later, Nas came walking out of the house.

"Yo, we gone have to watch out for her dude. He's not gonna just keep getting his ass kicked and not try to come for us. Besides, now he knows you've been knee-deep in his girl, trust me it's not over. Priest talked to her and told her we need to keep an eye on her, and it's best that she comes back to Philly for a little while. I think she's planning to stay with him," Nas stated, and that shit ain't gone work for me.

"Nah, she's staying with me, and that's the end of that," I snapped.

"Nigga, how you gone move her in with you, and you got

your girl? What you gone have your maybe baby mama, and your girl there at the same damn time?" Nas burst out laughing.

"If it comes down to that. I won't be fucking with Tiff anymore, but she's staying until we can figure out if that's my kid she's carrying. Dena has her own crib. I don't think her and Tiff will be around each other much," I said to him.

"So, you're done with Tiff? That's some bullshit and you know it! You might as well end that shit with Dena because it's about to be some shit at your crib. You know Dena a messy ass chick, and Tiff don't play. She gone beat Dena's ass," Nas laughed and Shawn was nodding his head in agreeance.

"Bro, I think it's the wrong move. Maybe you should put Tiff in a house somewhere. I don't think it's a good move to bring her to your house. She's pregnant and shouldn't be stressed out. I've been trying to call Brittany's phone, and I think she's sending me to voicemail. Can you track her location for me?" Shawn asked, and we walked to the car so that I could grab my laptop. He gave me her number and I ran it to get her location.

"She's at 1309 Buena Vista Ave, that's her address," I stated.

"How you know that's her address?" Nas smirked.

"Because when Tiff...Nigga, fuck you!" We all burst out laughing. That's what the fuck I do, I find people. Of course, I knew where Tiff was laying her head when she moved here.

"Man, you crazy as fuck with your stalking ass." Nas shook

his head, laughing at me. A few minutes later, Priest and Tiff came walking out of the house.

"Yo, I need y'all to drop me off to that address," Shawn spoke, and we all got into the truck.

Chapter Fourteen

SHAWN

I came out here to make sure shit was good with baby girl, and she wasn't trying to answer my calls. I've called her all times of the night and her ass didn't have a problem picking up before. Out of courtesy, I dialed her number again as we pulled into her driveway.

"What are we doing at Britt's house?" Tiff questioned, and it sounded as if her ass was a lil' nervous.

"I came here to make sure y'all was good, and now I need to lay eyes on her. Is there something I need to know before I go up in here?" I asked her because if she had a nigga in here, I guess we will be getting acquainted real soon.

"Umm, I don't live here," she spoke, pulling her phone out, and my brother took it, sticking it in his pocket.

"Give me my shit back!" She yelled.

"Don't you see that baby girl is sleep? Bro, you need me to let you in?" He asked as I got out of the truck.

"Nah...You know what? Do your thing, big bro. It's too many cars in the driveway for my liking. Lil' mama only has one car; it's one too many out this bitch. I guess you don't know anything about that, huh?" I looked at Tiff. Cannon got out, grabbing his kit out of his bag, and three minutes later, I was inside.

"Call if you need us." My bro dapped me up and walked back to the truck. She had a pretty decent crib from what I could see. Walking upstairs, I could hear music playing, so I decided to follow the sound to one of the bedrooms. I assumed it was her room since it was the only room with double doors. I eased the door open, and baby girl was lying there sleeping in the arms of some nigga. They were sleeping so hard neither of them heard me come in the room. My first mind was to walk back out and not even trip off the shit with shorty. But the thug in my ass was like hell nawl nigga, show yo' ass! This bitch was talking all that shit about being with me, and now she wrapped up with the next nigga.

I spotted a chair in the corner of the room and took a seat as I pulled out my blunt and lit it up. I sat there and got faded for an hour watching these niggas until Britt started to stir in her sleep. She finally crawled her naked ass out of bed and was about to go to the bathroom until she noticed me sitting in the corner. She screamed, and her dude jumped up, and I just sat there looking at these idiots.

"Yo, who the fuck are you?! And what the fuck you want?"
Dude asked.

"Nigga, sit yo' punk ass down, I came here to talk to Ms.
Lady over there. What's up, Baby girl?" I spoke, and Britt
turned the light on. I could tell that she hadn't realized who I
was, because the only little bit of light was coming from the
bathroom.

"Shawn! Oh fuck, wha...What are you doing out here?"
She stuttered.

"Yo, get this pussy out of here before I change my mind
and beat his ass," I said to her. We weren't gone talk about
shit with his ass standing here.

"Pussy?! I got your pussy, nigga!" I laughed because this
nigga sounded like a bitch. I can tell he wasn't a street nigga,
and he didn't understand that he was playing with his life. I
was listening to *For Your Glory-By Tasha Cobbs* on the flight
over. I'm feeling a little generous right now, so I'mma let him
rock out on that one. He better know that Tasha saved his
life!

"Tre, I need to talk to him. Can you please leave, and I will
call you? Thank you so much for bailing me out, and I will get
the money back to you later today," she told him. The nigga
act like he didn't want to go, so I pulled my gun out and sat it
on my lap.

"See, this the bullshit I'm talking about, I thought we
were going to figure this shit out. Yet, you got this nigga
walking up in here like he the shit. Nah, you keep that change
and lose my fuckin' number. I will never fight a nigga over

bitch that's for everybody!" He yelled in her face and walked out, putting his clothes on. I had to laugh at this clown ass nigga 'cause he was pissed the fuck off.

"Bitch! You not gone disrespect me because you know I will fuck you up!" She yelled, and he just turned and walked out. That was the smartest move dude could have made.

"So, you were trying to work shit out with your nigga, huh? I'm not gone lie when I walked in here and saw you laid up with that nigga, I was trying to figure out what was the best way to kill y'all asses. But as I was sitting here getting faded, I thought about it. I can't be one-sided, we're not together, and I've bust a few backs out since the last time I saw you. A nigga like me love to fuck, and I need pussy every day. Shit is hard for me and my lil' nigga out here in these streets. So, it's not fair to come down on you when you live out here, and I live in Philly. You should've kept that shit gutta and got it how you live it. Stop telling me shit when you not ready to make that move, and I can understand you wanting to take your time.

Now had we made shit official, both of you niggas would be on the morning news as a double homicide. A nigga on his grown man shit right now, and I'm passing out blessings. You need to thank God for looking over your life. I heard you were in trouble, and I wanted to come out here and check on you. I see you've had your legs open like the 7-11, I can clearly see that you're good. I'm going back to my hotel and get some sleep." I wanted shorty, but after seeing her with ole boy, I can't crawl up in the pussy and go to sleep.

"Shawn, it wasn't like that. I didn't sleep with him and I'm sorry you saw that. He came and bailed me out of jail and had been waiting on me for a while. I just told him he could sleep over because it was late." She felt the need to explain.

"Ms. Lady, you don't have to explain yourself. I'm tired as fuck, and I will probably spend most of my day sleeping. I know we're leaving here later tonight, so I will hit your line before we head out. Oh, yeah, Tiff is moving back to Philly for a little while. I know y'all have a business together." I ordered an Uber and walked outside to wait.

"Shawn! I will take you to your hotel. Please, I don't want our friendship to end like this." She ran out of the house with just a t-shirt on.

"This isn't ending our friendship; I just don't want your ass near me with another nigga on you. You gone have to get that nigga off you before we can chill. I appreciate the ride to my hotel," I told her and canceled my Uber. By the time we made it to the hotel, it was going on seven in the morning.

"If I take a shower, can I come in? I swear to you I haven't had sex since I came to visit you last." I looked at her for a minute, and even though she was lying in the bed with ole dude, I believed her and decided to let her come up with me. When I got out of the shower, I ordered some breakfast for us.

"I'm going to jump in the shower." She smiled.

"Yeah, you do that." I climbed into bed and it wasn't long before I drifted off to sleep. I felt a cool breeze hit my dick and the sensation like I was about to bust a nut. That shit had me ready to tear some pussy up. Opening my eyes, Brittany was in between my legs giving me that sloppy head.

"Shit, girl! Suck that muthafucka!" I gritted. The way her head was bobbing up and down and the grip she had on my dick was about to make my ass explode.

"Mmm, hmmm, bust in my mouth, baby." Shiiiddd, she didn't have to tell me twice. She was deep throating my dick so good, cum shot out of me so fast and hard. I thought I was going to choke her ass.

"Gotdamn!" I gritted. Once I gathered my composure, I got up, grabbing the condoms out of my bag and sheathing my dick. Pulling her to the edge of the bed, I rubbed my dick up and down her slit.

"Ohhhh shit!" She screamed as I dug in her walls. Lil' mama was gone pay for having that nigga in her crib.

"Shut up and take this dick!" I gritted, slamming into her ass over and over again.

"Shawn! Pull out! Oh God, it's too much! I can't take it!"

"Nahhh, you been showing your ass lately. Got that nigga laying up in yo' shit like that's your man. You been fucking him, Britt?" I was so deep in her pussy, it felt like I touched her damn rib cage.

"No! I promise I didn't. I've only been with you. Oh my God, it feels so good!" She moaned. I pulled out of her and flipped her over to hit it from the back. She gripped my dick as I slid inside of her, pounding the hell out of her pussy.

"Damn, this some good pussy," I growled.

"Shawn, please pull out! It's hurting me!" She cried and I stopped moving.

"Baby girl, you good?" I asked her because she was sitting here in tears.

"No, I'm in pain, and my stomach is killing me." I felt bad because she seemed like she was in a lot of pain.

"Do you want to go to the emergency room?" I asked her as I rubbed her stomach.

"No, I just want to lay here, and hopefully it will go away." I cleaned myself up and left out to go get her something to take for the pain. My phone was going off and I saw that it was my brother calling.

"What up?" I answered.

"Ma just called me and said Cedes moved out," he sighed.

"Man, I talked to Mercedes, and she told me she wasn't gone move in with his ass. I will get up with her when we get back. What time are we heading back?" I asked him.

"Everybody is tired, we're going to leave tomorrow. Tiff has to handle some business before she leaves, so you're good." He sounded stressed the fuck out.

"I'm already at the hotel, and Brittany is with me, but she's not feeling well. I will catch up with y'all later, I'm going back to bed." I ended the call with my brother and grabbed the shit that I needed from the hotel gift shop.

Chapter Fifteen

TIFF

I can't believe all the shit that was going on right now. I find out that my fiancé is a lying piece of shit, I'm pregnant and don't know whose damn baby I'm having. If that ain't some hoe shit, I don't know what is. I have a lot of things to figure out when it comes to Aniya seeing her dad and her grandmother. Cannon is pissed and he hasn't said much to me since we got to the hotel. He wouldn't let me get my own room. I tried going into the room with Nas or Priest and he was raising hell about that. After my shower, I stepped into the room and was shocked to see him holding and feeding my daughter.

"She woke up crying while you were in the shower."

"Thank you for getting her for me." I smiled because he was so attentive with her. It was as if she calmed him. I walked over to take her from him, and he didn't want me to take her.

"I ordered you lunch; it's on the table." He nodded in the direction of the food, and I walked over to eat. I hope Aniya goes back to sleep because I was still exhausted, and it was only one in the afternoon. I could feel him staring a hole through me, and I turned to look at him because he never stopped staring.

"What?" His stare was making me uncomfortable.

"Were you ever gonna tell me?" He questioned as he stood to put the baby in her travel crib.

"Yes, I just found out yesterday right before I got into the fight with Marlo. Cannon, I was going to call you. I just needed time to process it all. I was in shock. Not knowing who the father of your child is, is a messed-up situation to be in. I know you don't trust me, but I would never put either of us through that again. It was the worst mistake of my life."

"You're right, I don't trust you. If dude didn't fuck up and you were sure that baby was mine, I can almost bet that you would've been at the closest abortion clinic. So, no, I don't trust your ass, and that's why you're staying with me until we found out for sure." His words cut deep, and there was nothing for me to say. I got up and went into the bathroom because I couldn't hold back the tears. There was a time where this man would have given me anything, and I fucked it up.

I got myself together and walked out of the bathroom. He was still sitting in the same spot. Walking over to check on my baby, she was peacefully sleeping. Mentally I was drained, and I just needed to get my mind right. I was hurt yet again, putting my trust into another nigga that wasn't shit. I know Cannon may think I deserve the shitty ass attitude that he's giving me, and he might be right. It's just not the right time, and if this is what I have to deal with being with him, he can forget about me staying in his house.

"Yo, why the hell are you calling me when we were just texting? I told you I will be home tomorrow night, and after I'm done handling my business, I'm coming straight to you." I heard him speak, and it sounded as if he was talking to a woman. When he said that he loved her validated that he was indeed talking to a woman. I had no idea that he was involved with anyone. I felt a rush of anger come over me, I didn't even want to be in the room with him right now. I jumped up, putting my shoes on, and walked out of the room without saying shit to him. I had no right to be mad, but I was pissed! I needed to vent, so I called Cas.

"Hey, you alright?" She asked.

"I'm good, just in my feelings a little bit. I just found out that Cannon has a girl, and for some reason, that shit pissed me off," I said to her.

"Tiff, what did you expect him to do? You went back to Cali to live your life with your man and baby. You made a choice that didn't include him. Hell, you did a lot of shit that didn't include him. Some of the shit I don't understand, and I'm not the one to sugar coat this shit for you. You were wrong, sis, and nothing is going to change the fact that you fucked up. I'm not going to keep beating you over the head about it, but you know damn well you can't be mad at him. I've never known Cannon to play second best to nobody. Let me tell you how God showed out on this one.

You came home with your man and new baby, you end up in bed with the man that your heart really belongs to, and then go back to your life on some settling shit with puss boy. The reason you're pregnant now and the reason you caught bitch boy on his ain't shit nigga shit, is only because God stepped in. Well, God doesn't condone cheating, this was an emergency and I'm glad he showed up. Now, Cannon wants you to come live with him until y'all can find out if that's his baby. Girl, you better go up in that muthafuckin' house and show the fuck out. Dena is there because he's settling. You bruised his heart. She's a placement holder until his true desire could get her shit together. Walk around that bitch half damn naked if you have to. Tell his ass clothes give you the hives or some shit. Now, if your confused ass still don't know what you want, leave him alone and let him move on. Keep that wicked ass pussy to yourself, bihhh! Got this nigga out here losing his damn mind. I gotta go, my man is calling me. I will see you tomorrow." She didn't even give me time to respond; she just hung up. Just as I was about to go back into the room, I saw Shawn walking out of his room, carrying a girl in his arms.

"Oh, shit! Britt, what's wrong?" I ran up to them because she was screaming that she was in pain.

"This nigga and his dick is what's wrong! Girl, if you know

what's best for you, don't fuck Cannon. These niggas is on some hateful ass revenge type shit! Got me out here about to be pussyless. Go back to the other side, sis, where fuckin' with bitches is safe... Argggggghhhhh!" She screamed and Shawn was shaking his head.

"I'm taking her to see her doctor. We will call you when we get back," he spoke.

"Bro, what's going on?" I heard Cannon ask from behind me.

"She's not feeling well. I will call y'all as soon as we get back to the room." He rushed off with Brittany still going off, and I couldn't help but laugh at her crazy ass. Turning to walk back into the room, he grabbed my arm and pinned me against the wall.

"Lose the attitude. You created this shit, now deal with it." Jerking out of his embrace, I walked back inside of our room and laid down for a nap.

Chapter Sixteen
BRITTANY

I almost shitted on myself seeing Shawn in my damn house. That crazy ass nigga could have killed us. What I said to him was the truth, I didn't sleep with Tre, and I'm happy as hell that neither of them acted a fool. I could only imagine what the fuck would have happened if we were in the bed fucking. When we got back to his hotel, I thought we were cool until we started fucking.

These niggas don't play fair, and even though the dick was feeling good. My pussy was screaming. The more I yelled stop, the more this nigga drove his dick into my esophagus. I knew I should have left that fuckin' leg he calls a dick alone, but nooooooo. A bitch wants to be sucking and slobbering, trying to get the nigga back on her good side. Now my ass is paying for that shit. We just left the doctor's office, and this nigga done bruised my fuckin' cootie cat and all the shit that comes along with it. The doctor said that my cervix is bruised. He said it will heal, but we need to take it easy. What in the big dick Willie shit is this! I've heard of women talking about getting hurt by having rough sex. I just never thought it would be my ass.

"From now on, I'm not giving you no pussy. We just gonna have to skin hump. Rub your dick between my thighs and imagine that shit is my pussy. Nigga, you done ruined my ass. Now I gotta soak my pussy three times a day all because you got a dinosaur dick and you a messy nigga!" I was going the hell off, and this nigga was sitting here with this dumb ass smirk on his face.

"Bruh, calm down. I wasn't revenge fuckin' you. I told you I was good on the shit that happened back at your house. I'm sorry if I was a little too rough. I promise I will kiss it when we get back to the room. But all the bullshit about skin bumping and fucking your thighs is a no for me. I'm fuckin' wet, gushy pussy every day! I'mma give you a pass tonight." He smiled.

"Nahhh, I'm good." I pulled my vibrating phone out, and it was a text message from Tre.

Tre: *That was some foul shit you pulled. I was gone let the shit go, but fuck that, you a disrespectful ass bitch! You better watch your fuckin back, stupid bitch!*

This nigga got me fucked up. I knew if I told Shawn about the text, it would be some shit. So, I just let it go for now. We picked up some food and went back to his room to eat and relax. We heard a knock at the door, and Shawn went to answer it.

"Hey, I was just coming to check on Brittany." I heard Tiff speak, and I forgot to call her when we got back.

"Y'all go ahead and talk, I'm about to go next door and talk to my brother," Shawn told her and left out.

"Girl, what the fuck happened?" Tiff asked, sitting down in the chair.

"Bihhhh, this nigga tore my shit up!" I couldn't do shit but laugh.

"I tried to warn your ass that he was coming in your house, Cannon took my damn phone. Was Tre in the house with you?" She questioned.

"Hell yeah! My ass was lying in bed butt ass naked. Shawn didn't show his ass. This crazy nigga sat and watched us sleep on some fatal attraction type shit, the nigga edition. Bruh had my ass shook, sis! A bitch put on her knee pads and went to work on that nigga. I thought we were cool until that death-stroke let my ass know what type time we were really on. And if I'm getting dick out the ears, bruh, your dick lashing is gone be some other type of shit." We both burst out laughing.

"I think I'm good! He has a girl now, so I'm not sure why the fuck he wants me to stay in his house. Priest thinks that it's best that I come back to Philly for a little while. Zoey and I spoke a few minutes ago, and she said that they have tests that they can do to determine DNA before you give birth. I'm going to do that just as soon as the doctor says it's safe." I felt bad for her because I knew her true feelings for Cannon.

For months I watched her cry over what she had done to him and the pain she was feeling because she loved him. The only reason she moved on is that she knew he wanted nothing to do with her.

"Girl, you better put on your best thong and twerk on that dick. Fuck that hoe!" This girl started gyrating in her chair, and we fell out laughing, not realizing that Shawn and Cannon both were in the room as he held Aniya in his arms.

For the rest of the night, we all chilled and watched some movies. Tiff and I had to handle some business regarding our shop because I decided to go back to Philadelphia with them for a while. Thank God we have Kelly running the shop for us. She's dope, and I trust that she will keep things together.

Chapter Seventeen

NAS

"Get that shit, Bear! I missed your sexy ass," I groaned, watching my wife ride the hell out of my dick.

"Ahhh, I missed you...Oh shit!" She screamed as I stroked the hell out of her pussy.

"Yeah, you like that shit, don't you, Bear?!"

"Mmm hmmmm. Shit, I'm about to cum!" She moaned and we both released together.

"Fuck! Bear, I swear if you wasn't already pregnant, you would be after that bucket of cum I just dropped in yo' ass." She turned her damn head so quick, I thought that shit was gone crack.

"Pregnant! Nigga, don't be wishing that shit on us. We have New York and Paris Fashion week coming up. I don't have time to be sick when we have so much to do to get

Zoey and Sasha ready." She had her face all frowned the hell up.

"Bear, I know pregnant pussy when I feel it, and that cat box you got down there is the fuck pregnant. Gone to the Walgreens and get you a pregnancy test or call the doctor and set up an appointment because you damn sure gone need it. Damn! My bear 'bout to have me another baby." I smiled, and she nudged me on the arm.

"Nooooo! Babe, we can't have a baby right now," she whined.

"Well, ya fast ass should've kept yo' legs closed," I laughed because baby girl was pouting something serious.

"Babe, how you think Cannon and Tiff did on their first night in the same house?" Cas asked.

"I don't know but me and Big Mama going over there to see how Tiff holding up. I should make his ass throw something on the grill and send Dena an anonymous text inviting her over. I wanna see all the action they got going on over there." I bust out laughing 'cause that shit would be epic.

"You a messy nigga, you and Big Mama going over there to be damn nosey. Y'all don't give a damn how she's holding up. But I'm here for all the messy shit," she stated, and we fell out in laughter.

"Is Sasha excited about doing fashion week with her mom?" I asked because I thought that was the dopest shit. Zoey was asked to do New York Fashion week by this new designer, and she asked her if Sasha could do it as well. Cas ass hurried and put Sash under her management company.

When it comes to Zoey and her children, my brother doesn't bother her. He's been trying to get Zoe to take a vacation without the kids for a year now, and that shit ain't happening. It's always them, the kids, and their nanny! Fuck that, Cas and I need a break from that lil' damn terror we got running around here.

"Yes, she is, and I'm excited that the family is all going to New York to see her do her thing. I swear that photoshoot she and Zoe did has been getting them all kinds of contracts," She smiled. Just as I was about to go hop in the shower, my phone was going off.

"Yeah."

"Yo, have you talked to Cannon?" Priest asked.

"Nah, not yet. I was going over to his crib in a couple of hours. Why what's up?" I asked.

"Tiff just called me and said Cannon was snapping out. Something about Mercedes boyfriend beat her son so bad, he's in a coma." I couldn't believe what the fuck my brother was saying right now.

"What the fuck! You can't be serious." I knew Cannon and Shawn were about to tear this fuckin' city down. And I will be right by there with them, this nigga put his hand on a fuckin' child!

"They're at Jefferson hospital, I just left the shop, and I'm on my way there now. I will see you when you get there." He hung up, and I hurried to get myself together.

"Babe, what's going on?" Cas asked, stepping into the shower.

"Cedes n

coma." That

"Oh my

I know Ms.

boy," she s

some cloth

had a doze

hospital, it

"Bro, t

this," Prie

"I put

Cannon r

"Noo⌣, ⌣⌣⌣

talked to him to get his side of the story." If I was a wo...... ,

would beat the shit out of Mercedes right now.

"His side! His muthafuckin' side! That little boy lying up in that fuckin' hospital bed fighting for his got damn life is all the fuckin' side you need!" Shawn barked.

"Cedes, you sound fucking stupid right now. You care more about that bum ass nigga than you do about your own fucking son! I'm gone need you to help me understand that shit 'cause when I'm giving out these muthafuckin hollow tips, I want to make sure I have one for your weak ass! I don't give a fuck about you being my sister. If you're siding with that pussy ass nigga, that means you against my nephew. 'Cause I'm telling you now that nigga gone die today! I don't give a fuck who hears me, I don't give a fuck about no cops, and I damn sure don't give a fuck about what

you got going on. If that shit ain't

shit we need to be discussing

stand on that shit." I could

was with him. If he's go

a killing spree.

"Y'all stop it!

wrong with yo

quick! The

to you

here

about Jeremiah, there ain't
. Pick yo' poison, lil' sis, and
understand Cannon's anger and I
ng on a killing spree, we all going on

Mercedes, I don't know what the fuck is
u, but your ass better get some sense in you real
e isn't a man alive that should be more important
than your child. You running your black ass around
defending that piss poor ass nigga! He's a low life bitch
or what he did to my grandbaby, and if your brothers don't
get to his ass first, I promise you I'm gone kill his ass myself
and make your dumb ass watch! I tried to tell you about that
boy, and you argued me down about him. All I know is that
when my grandson pulls through, I'm beating your ass.

You can count on that ass whipping. Daughter or not, you
gone have to see me just for playing in my damn face with this
dumb ass shit. And when I'm done, I will help you clean yourself up. Now, boys, I need for y'all to get your shit together
and calm down up in these people hospital. Y'all asses can't
do nothing behind bars." Damn Ma B. wasn't playing with
her ass

"Shiddd! My reach long behind bars or not, that nigga can
and will be touched," Cannon spoke, walking out the door
mad as hell. Priest, Shawn, and I walked out behind him.

"We with y'all, bro. Just say the word and we there," I told
him. Whatever he wanted to do and whenever he was ready
to do it, Priest and I were going to be right there with them.

Mercedes came running out of the hospital, headed towards the parking lot.

"Yo, I bet she going to that nigga." Shawn started jogging to his car, and we were right behind him.

"We need to go in my car," Cannon yelled as he popped the trunk and tossing Shawn the keys. We all jumped in, and he pulled his laptop out to track Cedes down because she sped out of the parking lot so damn quick.

"This that dumb shit I'm talking about with her ass. She should be in that damn hospital with her son. She out here looking like a fraud ass bitch right now!" I hope Mercedes had nothing to do with this mess. Because that would put everyone in a fucked-up situation.

"She's on seventy-six, it looks like she's headed to Roosevelt Blvd," Cannon spoke as he hooked his computer to some shit he had in his car. If I didn't know that this nigga pushed dope, I would swear he was some special ops type of nigga for the police. Pulling up a few cars down from Mercedes' car. We got out, and Cannon popped his trunk, pressing the button to the gun compartment he had inside. Pulling my gun out waiting for them to strap up, I never leave home without my bitch. We walked up on the steps, and Cannon messed with the locks. A couple of minutes later, we were moving inside. We could here Mercedes crying and yelling.

"Why would you do my son like that, Samir?! Spanking him is one thing, but you beat my baby half to death!" She cried.

"I just lost it, baby. That lil' nigga was just doing too much and I lost it. I'm sorry, you have to know that I'm sorry. Do you forgive me?" He asked Mercedes.

"I don't know if I can forgive you for this. My family will never forgive me, and regardless of what everyone thinks, I love my son. You have to get out of town because my brothers are going to kill you. I don't want to see you dead, so you need to get out of town," she told him and I just shook my head.

"Man, I done told you before, I'm not scared of your fuckin' brothers! If them niggas want to see me, they can bring that shit! Fuck them niggas!" That was all Cannon needed to hear, and kicked the bedroom door opened.

"Oh shit! Bry, please don't kill him," Cedes cried, but it was too late for that shit. Just as sure as my name is Nasir, this nigga is dead. My nigga never pulls his gun out and not let that bitch sing. Somebody gone get that heat, and Cedes better move her ass out the way before this nigga really forget she's his sister.

"Nigga, why you got that gun on me? I didn't do that shit!" This nigga, Samir, bellowed.

"Hold up, Bry! This pussy like to beat kids; he needs to feel the same shit my nephew felt when he put his hands on him. Then you can pop his ass! My nephew is three years old, pussy!" Shawn spazzed out, sending blow after blow to that nigga's face. Shawn beat this dude ass so bad you could hear bones cracking.

"Noooooo! Shawn, please, you have to stop before you kill him!" Mercedes cried while Priest held onto her.

"Shawn! That's enough," Cannon called out, and when his brother moved, it was no rap, he lit that nigga up. I had to make myself useful, so I made the call to the cleanup crew, and it took about twenty minutes for them to get here. Shawn guided their sister to Cannon's car while Priest and I drove her car back to the hospital.

Chapter Eighteen
CANNON

I don't know what the fuck is wrong with my sister. She was still acting like a damn fool over that nigga, but she knew not to play with me. I can't believe she was gone let that nigga rock out after what he did to Jeremiah. Nah, that shit will never go down like that. My nephew was still in a coma, and the doctors say they don't believe he will pull through. My family serves a higher power, and God has the last word. So, I'm gone keep believing that he will be alright.

"Son, why don't you go home and get some sleep? I will call you if anything changes," my mother spoke and I decided to listen. It was almost eight in the morning. After we took care of that piece of shit ass nigga, I came back to the hospital with my mom, and Shawn took Mercedes back to his house.

"Ok, Ma. I will be back later, so you can go home and get some rest." I kissed her cheek.

"No, I'm not leaving until he does. I'm fine right here, I'm going to sleep on this stretch out couch. Thank you for making sure he has a private room, and I'm comfortable." I had to make sure that she would be good, and I wanted Jeremiah in a room by himself. I said my goodbyes and left out. It took me about thirty minutes to get home, and when I pulled into my driveway, Dena's car was here. I let out an exasperated sigh and got out of the car. This is the first time that Dena and Tiff would meet. I know her ass coming over unannounced is to be on some messy shit that I didn't have time for. Getting out of my car, she was already waiting for me.

"Hey, babe. How are you holding up? I wanted to come and check on you and cater to my man for the day." She smiled.

"Why didn't you call me?" I asked her.

"I wanted to surprise you and bring you some breakfast." She held the bag up, leaning in to kiss my lips. Walking into the house, I could hear Tiff laughing, Dena, and I walked into the kitchen, and she was on the phone.

"Britt, let me call you back," she stated.

"Ok, boo. Remember what I said put yo' best thong..." Tiff hurried and ended the call and turned to Dena and me.

"Hey, I'm Tiffany, and you are?" She smiled at Dena.

"His girl is all you need to know," Dena snapped.

"Oh, hmmm, mmmkk... Cannon, I made breakfast. Would

you like some?" Tiff ignored her comment, which surprised the hell out of me.

"He's good, I know you see this food in my hand." Dena was getting disrespectful, and Tiff was getting pissed.

"I'm good, Tiff. Dena! Cut that shit out and bring yo' ass on. All that shit isn't even necessary," I told her. She was gone make me snatch her ass up. There was no need to introduce the two because Dena fucked that up, and I knew Tiff wasn't feeling how she came at her. She may not have shown it then, but I was damn sure gone hear about it later. I went to take a quick shower and crawled in bed. I was so damn tired I drifted off as soon as my head hit the pillow. I heard a knock on my door, and I looked at the clock; it was going on nine at night. Fuck! I didn't mean to sleep all damn day Dena was still sleeping. I got out of bed and went to answer the door. When I did, I wanted to shut that shit back and go back to bed cause baby girl was being messy as fuck right now. Tiff was standing here in a thong and bra eating a pint of damn ice cream.

"Didn't mean to wake you, but Shawn is trying to reach you." She smirked. Instead of her ass leaving, she stood there licking her damn spoon. Before I could say anything, Dena was already on go, I didn't even hear her get out of bed.

"Cannon, I know this bitch isn't standing here naked," Dena snapped, and my ass was still stuck, looking at Tiff's fine ass.

"Bitch! Be mindful when you call me a bitch. I hate that word when it's directed at me. I eat bitches like you for dinner, don't fuck around and get your ass tore up in here in front of your man. That shit would be embarrassing, and one thing about me, I will embarrass yo' ass. Now, clothes irritate the fuck out of me, and when I'm in the comfort of my home, I need to be comfortable," Tiff spat.

"This ain't your damn home, you just here until we can find out if that's my man's baby. You should be ashamed of yourself walking around and don't know who your baby daddy is!" Dena screamed.

"Dena, shut the hell up, and Tiff, go put some damn clothes on." I wasn't trying to hear this shit.

"I'm not putting on shit as a matter of fact. Fuck this girl! I'm not ashamed of shit. I enjoyed every moment of sliding down on your man's dick! If I was you, I would be worrying about if I'm gone slide down on it again." Tiff turned and walked away with her fat ass bouncing all over the place. All I could do is shake my damn head.

"I'm not doing this shit with you, muthafucka. You better find her another place to go. You told me everything would be cool, but this bitch talking that shit about sliding down on your dick and walking around here half damn naked and shit. You better do something about it, or I will," she spazzed out.

"Girl, sit yo' ass down. This is my shit, and you need to understand that. Tiff was out of line, and so was your ass! She knows we together because I told her we were. I'm not hiding shit from you, but you gone stop being disrespectful up in here 'cause she's not going anywhere." I was sick of this shit already. I walked down the hall in search of Tiff's ass, and she was walking back upstairs. Grabbing her up, I pushed her against the wall.

"Stop fuckin' playing with me. You're doing too much, walking around here with no damn clothes on. I'm gone make sure she's respectful, but understand that you're going to do the same when my girl is here." And she burst out laughing like this shit was a game.

"You sound like you meant that shit, baby. I'mma do what the fuck I want, you can either let me go over to my mom's or I'm gone be walking around this bitch butt ass naked every day." When she ran her tongue across my lip, I almost forgot I had a girl and sucked that bitch into my mouth. She walked away, and I was still standing there stuck. This may have been a bad fuckin' idea. Walking back to my room, Dena was pacing back and forth like a madwoman.

"She has to go, fuck her being pregnant! I'm supposed to be your woman and you got this bitch up in here doing what the fuck she wants, like this her shit! It's going to be me or her. Fuck all that other shit!" Now she knew not to give me no damn ultimatum.

"I'mma let you think about what you just said. I had a talk with her about the disrespect, but your ass ain't no better. Oh, and she's not going anywhere until I know what it is. If that shit don't work for you, then you gone have to do what you need to do. Now I'm about to leave and go check on my mom," I said to her and walked into the bathroom to hop in the shower. Dena ass has been knowing me for a long time, and she knows I don't do well with idle threats. I'm gone let her have this one because she's upset. After my shower, I walked back into my bedroom to get dressed, and her ass had crawled back into bed.

"What are you doing?" I questioned, and I threw my clothes on.

"I'm staying here until you get back, I'm too tired to drive home." I knew that was a bad idea but decided to let her stay. I didn't have time to argue with her, Shawn had been calling, and I needed to make sure everything was good.

*I*t was game on with that bitch. I was planning to be respectful and stay out the way when she was here with Cannon. This bitch up in here talking shit. Man, fuck that girl! I was trying to keep the old Tiff suppressed, this bitch tried it and I'm gone finish that shit.

"Girl, this shit is hilarious! Bitch, you went and knocked on the door in yo' best muthafuckin' thong! You had that V Secret on for that bihhhh, huh? Wheww, I wish I was there to see that shit." Britt fell out laughing again.

"I can only imagine the look on his fuckin' face. I don't even know if I would put on a thong and bra. That nigga would be so damn tired of seeing my naked ass he gone either put me out or fuck me," Cas spoke, and we burst out laughing.

"Hell yeah, girl. He was stuck like a muthafucka. By the

time I'm done, he gone be ready to take my ass to my mama's house," I spoke, and we both fell out laughing.

"Wheewww, baby, your petty runs deep. Just remember who you playing with. That nigga isn't named Cannon for nothing; that muthafucka is crazy as fuck. Bruh, that revenge fuck he gone put on yo' ass when he finally realizes he with the wrong chick. Hunntyyy, y'all not gone have to worry about the doctor delivering the baby, he gone fuck it out of you. Got my shit hurting again, just thinking about what you got coming your way," she stated.

"I don't have to worry about that. He's too wrapped up into her ass. Let me call you back in a few, I need to go feed Aniya." Britt and I ended the call, and I walked upstairs to my bedroom but stopped when I heard this hoe talking shit about me.

"Girl, this bitch gone make me beat her ass in here! I be damn if she gone fuck up what I got going." She had the call on speaker because I could hear the chick laughing.

"Bitch, y'all got some shit going on over there. Get your money, girl. You better hope that Cannon and Rob never find out about each other. I don't know why you wanted to get in some shit with Cannon if you and Rob were still together anyway. That shit gone blow up in your face all because you trying to get a bag," the girl said to Dena, and my interest was fuckin' piqued. I couldn't believe what I was hearing.

"I got this shit under control. Cannon don't have time to be worrying about what the fuck I'm doing, and Rob too busy being pussy whipped to care. Anyhoo, let me go relax in my man's bed, and I will call you tomorrow." They ended their call, and I tiptoed into my room. I couldn't wait to call Britt ass and tell her what the fuck I just heard. My phone was going off and it was Marlo calling me for the hundredth time. I knew I would have to eventually talk to him. I wasn't ready to talk to his ass right now though. My phone was going off again, and I thought it was him calling back, but it was my mom.

"Hey, Ma."

"Hey, I just wanted to check on you and Niya. How Cannon treating y'all over there?" She asked.

"Ma, you have to come over here and talk to him. I think it's best that I stay with you," I told her.

"Girl, your ass act like you over there being held hostage. You a grown damn woman and can't no man make you stay where you don't want to stay. Yo' ass over there 'cause your hot coochie box ass want to be. I feel you though, that man is something serious to look at. Did you meet the lil' girlfriend already?" She questioned.

"Yeah, and the bitch tried me," I sighed.

"Well, try not to beat her ass. You have to remember you're pregnant. I'm coming to pick my granddaughter up tomorrow; I don't want her caught up in no bullshit." I think my mom is right. It may be best that she come and get Niya for a few days. We talked for a few more minutes and ended the call. Walking downstairs to get my ice cream, I ran into Dena coming out of the kitchen.

"If you think for one minute that I'm going to let you

mess shit up for me, you got another thing coming. Cannon is all me, and as long as you know that, we gone be good," she spoke. This bitch was barking up the wrong tree.

"Yeah, I wouldn't want to mess up your bag! Tell Rob I said hi, bitch!" The look on her face was priceless. I had to let her ass know. Bitch, I will pull your fuckin' card. Don't play in my face. Funky ass hoe! Walking into the kitchen just as I grabbed my ice cream, I heard the front door open.

"Babeee!" This dramatic bitch yelled out, running and jumping in his arms, and he carried her into the kitchen. He was smiling in her face until he realized I was standing in the kitchen. I chuckled and walked off, heading back to my room for the night. I must have dozed off because I heard Aniya whining. When I sat up in bed, Cannon was sitting in the chair, feeding her.

"You're going to have to pump in the morning; she only has a few bottles left." He smiled down at Aniya and then looked at me.

"I will, how is Jeremiah?" I asked.

"He's still in a coma, the specialist that came in today gave my mom some good news. He believes that Jeremiah will pull through; he just may have some disabilities. I don't give a damn what he has wrong with him. He will have everything he needs. I just need my lil' guy to wake up," he spoke, and I felt bad for the family, especially Jeremiah. He's so pissed with his sister he wants nothing to do with her ass right now, and I can't blame him. I never knew that Cannon was so attentive when it came to kids, and now, I know why he reacted the way he did with our situation.

"I'm sorry you all are going through this. I'm here if you ever need to talk. Niya is going with my mom for a few days, so I will try to stay out of the way while your girl is here. She doesn't like me, and I damn sure can't get down with her ass. I don't want to cause extra drama for you while you're going through this with your nephew."

"I appreciate that. She went home, so you're good. One thing that you can do for me is put some clothes on. Like right now, why are you lying there like that? I believe you're determined to drive my ass crazy. I swear if I ever get a hold of you, I'm tearing your shit to shreds." He stood to put Aniya back in her crib and walked out without saying anything else. The next morning, I was up, getting things together for my mom to come and get her. Picking her up out of her bed and grabbing all of her bags, we went downstairs. Cannon was in the kitchen cooking breakfast.

"It smells good in here." I smiled, putting the baby in her swing.

"Have a seat and I will make your plate." He didn't have to tell my greedy ass twice. I sat down, and he placed the plate in front of me, and I wanted to kiss this nigga for real. I pulled my phone out, snapped a picture, and text it to Nas. Cannon burst out laughing at me, shaking his head.

"Y'all still do that greedy ass shit?" He asked.

"Don't judge us. It's a cousin thing and this is how we bond." I laughed as I stuffed my damn face. This was the first time that he and I actually shared a laugh in a long time, and it felt good. I started to say something about what I heard his girl talking about. I decided not to say shit and mind my damn business. All I know is her ass better not push me.

Nas: *Damn, that look good! This new cook looks like she gone be alright. I'm on my way.*

Me: *Nigga, I'm not at Priest house; Cannon cooked all of this for me.*

Nas: *Cannon! That nigga can't cook. Bruh, you better not eat that shit.*

Me: *Bye. Boy, I will call you later.* I fell out laughing at his dumb ass.

"What's so funny?" he looked over at me.

"Laughing at Nas. He said you can't cook and for me not to eat your food."

"Clearly, we know that's a lie. You have had plenty of my cooking. If that nigga ever found out that I can throw down in the kitchen, I would never get rid of him. So, it's best that he keeps believing that I can't cook. Baby girl, why must you continue to walk around my house half damn naked?" He asked.

"I was serious about needing to be comfortable, I don't like wearing clothes when I'm pregnant." I shrugged. I had to laugh on the inside because this shit was getting that nigga. I had on a tank top and thong all my ass was out, and that's just the way I wanted it.

"You really trying to make this shit hard for a nigga." He shook his head and got up to clean our plates. The doorbell sounded off and I knew that it was my mom. I didn't even bother putting on clothes when I answered the door.

"Girl, why the hell you half damn naked?!" She looked passed me, and I knew Cannon was standing behind me.

"Hey, Ms. Gabby. Come on in," he spoke, and she walked into the house.

"Damn! It's nice as hell in here. Boy, you got some taste, expensive taste at that. You got my daughter over here living good, I like that. Now, this is how a man is supposed to set his woman up. I see why yo' ass walking around here with nothing on," my mom stated, and I was so embarrassed.

"Thanks. Let me get baby girl for you," he said and walked back into the kitchen.

"Ma, I'm not his woman; he has a girl," I whispered.

"The keyword is girl, she ain't his wife, and by the way, he kept looking down at your ass, she won't be his girl long. Now, where is my grandbaby? We gone go ahead and leave, so y'all can play hide and damn seek. Lawwd, it don't make no sense for that man to look like that," she stated, just as Cannon came back with Niya and her bags.

"Her car seat is in my truck, I will get it for you," he told her.

"That's ok, I got everything I need, I just need the baby and plenty of breast milk. Tiff, I will call you if we need you to pump us some more," she said to me.

"I will probably come over and stay a couple of nights with you soon, mom," I yelled out.

"Nah, we don't need no company; stay yo' ass right here.

Lawd knows you need to stay right the hell here!" My mom didn't know what the hell to say out of her mouth. When I closed the door, I bumped right into his chest as he stared down at me.

"This is a volcano you don't want to play with, lil' mama."

"I love when volcanoes erupt, I think that shit is sexy as hell." I moved to the side and walked past him, putting some extra sway in my hips because I knew his ass was watching. Before I could make it to the top of the stairs, I was being lifted in the air, and the thong I had on was being ripped off of me. Wrapping my legs around his neck with my back pressed against the wall as he devoured my pussy. The way his tongue eased in and out of me was driving me crazy.

"Ohhhhhhh, shit!" I moaned as he latched on to my clit, sucking and licking so sensual yet so fuckin' aggressive. This nigga was hungry, and all I wanted to do was feed him.

"Damn, you taste good," he growled as I tried to push his head deeper into my center. I swear I've had head before; nothing compares to the way this dude gives it up. When he swirled his tongue, applying pressure to my clit, I could feel the buildup, and I knew I was about to cum.

"Cannon! Ahhhhhh! I can't hold it, shit!" I screamed, squeezing my damn thighs tighter around his head.

"Give me all that shit! Damn, this some sweet ass pussy." This man had my ass spent, as he sucked all the cum out of me. When he eased me down onto the floor, he kissed my lips and walked away. My pussy was on fire and this nigga just walks away.

"What are you doing?" I yelled out to him.

"I can't fuck you, babe. It would be wrong of me to do that to Dena." I know this nigga didn't just say that shit when his lips were just wrapped around my pussy.

"Nigga! Did you give a fuck about me when I told you I was engaged and couldn't do it a few months back? No, you didn't give two fucks. You were sticking your dick so far up my ass the shit was coming out my ears! Now you're sitting here trying to be faithful to a bitch that ain't faithful to your ass! Nah, bruh, unless you want me to go fuck another nigga, you gone give my pregnant horny ass some dick!" I was so damn mad I didn't realize that I had slipped up and told on the bitch.

"What the fuck you just say?! How do you know that she's not faithful to me?" He questioned, walking up on me.

"Uhhhhh..."

"Answer the question! How do you know?" He was mad as hell, and I should have kept my mouth shut.

"I overheard her in your room talking on the phone with a friend," I whispered. He walked into his bedroom and slamming the door.

Chapter Twenty
CANNON

I was mad that Dena tried to play me. Something with us just didn't click for me, and It seemed that I was trying to force it. I cared for her, and I thought she was a cool chick; I just couldn't say that I was in love with her. The guys were right; I didn't have the woman I really wanted, so I settled. We could have kept the shit the way it was if she wanted to do her thing. She kept fuckin' with me about being in a relationship, and we had been fuckin' around for a couple of years, so I decided to give her what she wanted.

Tiff said that she heard her on the phone talking to her friend. It was easy for me to confirm by pulling up my camera recordings. I heard all I needed to hear and then some. Ever since that shit went down with Priest and Zoey, I made it a fact to get cameras installed all over my crib. You never know when they will come in handy. I even heard the whole Operation Cannon bullshit with Tiff, Britt, Zoey, and Cas. I had to chuckle at that shit. Lil' mama was trying to wear a nigga down. What's fucked up is, that shit was working. That's why my lips were wrapped around her fat ass pussy. Dena should have done something safe instead of fuckin' with a nigga like me. My phone was going off and my brother was calling.

"Yeah," I spoke.

"Bro, get down to the hospital." He hung up before I could even ask what was going on. Rushing out of the house, I headed to the hospital, praying that nothing happened to Jeremiah. It took me about thirty minutes to get to the hospital, and when I walked into his room, everyone was standing around his bed. I broke down because my lil' man was up trying to talk to his grandma. You can tell that he was weak, but he was awake, and I was so damn happy.

"Hey, lil' man. I'm glad to see you up." I smiled at him.

"He's weak, and they haven't run any mobility test on him yet. I'm just so damn happy he woke up," my mom stated as she wiped the tears from her eyes. I looked over at my sister, and she was sitting in a chair next to his bed holding his hand. I hope and pray that she gets her shit together for the sake of that little boy. After seeing all the shit that went on with her, it is best that Jerimiah stay with my mom. I guess mom knew what she was talking about.

"You good, bruh?" Shawn walked up to me.

"I found out that Dena is on some bullshit, other than that I'm good." He didn't even look shocked.

"Bro, she been on some bullshit. What you expected from

her ghetto ass? All Dena ass wanted was to run up a check. I tried to tell you this shit a while ago, which is why I never understood why you tried to wife her ass up," he spoke.

I stayed at the hospital with my family for a few hours. We all had a long talk with Mercedes, and she understood that when Jerimiah got released from the hospital, he was going to be with mom. We had a shipment come in, and I stopped by to check on that before I called it a night and went home. I shot Dena a text, letting her know that I wanted to see her. She quickly responded that she would be right over. I told her I would leave the door unlocked for her to come on in. Walking into the house, it was quiet. I guess Tiff was in her room. Walking past her door, I heard light moaning, and I just knew she didn't have a nigga in my shit. Easing her door open, baby girl was going to work on her pussy. She opened her eyes, watching me watch her as she continued to massage that fat ass clit. It was calling me, and I swear I couldn't walk away if I wanted to. Taking my clothes off and placing my gun on the bed, I immediately pulled her to the edge.

"Can I suck on your pussy, baby?" I slid my tongue across her mound as her back raised from the bed.

"Mmmmm hmmmmm, please suck it," She moaned.

"All I want is for you to cum in my fuckin' mouth," I spoke, pulling her clit into my mouth and sucking on that shit until it was numb as the cum rushed out of her.

"Oh fuck!" She screamed. Standing up, I turned on the soundbar in the room and *Work to Do by August Alsina* came blaring through the speaker.

"Cannon, please fuck me! I need you! I need you to fuck me now," she whimpered. Hearing her cry out begging for me, pushed me over the edge, causing me to enter her with force.

"Fuck! This pussy is a beast!" I gritted, thrusting deep into her, tearing her G-spot the fuck apart.

"Ahhhhhhh! Fuck me, baby! Shit!" She groaned, and I swear this pussy was so good a nigga was ready to explode.

"Come ride this dick, baby." I pulled out of her and sat on the bed. She eased down on me, bouncing and rocking her body back and forth on my shit. I gripped her ass cheeks, pounding the shit out of her walls.

"Ahhh shit! I'm cum...I'm cumming!" She screamed out.

"Fuck yeah! Urgghhhhh!" I roared, releasing a nut so hard I think my soul left with that shit.

"What the fuck are you doing!" Dena yelled out, which caused Tiff to jump off of me.

"It's called fuckin'. It was some of the best pussy I've ever had in my life too," I said to this bitch.

"Bitch, you fucked my man!" She tried to get at Tiff, but I snatched her ass up. With Tiff pussy juice all over my hands and wet dick swinging back and forth.

"Bitch, I'm not your man! You got a nigga and thought you were going to try and play me! Fuck you, go find that nigga Rob, and play with his ass. Now get the fuck out of my shit, and if you ever fuck with her, just know I will kill you," I gritted, releasing her ass.

"Cannon, that bitch is lying," she cried.

"Get the fuck out!" I roared, and she ran out of the room.

"Did you know she was coming over?" Tiff questioned.

"I did, but seeing how wet your pussy was fogged my memory," I replied and walked out of the room to make sure Dena's ass left my house and to lock up. When I made it back upstairs, Tiff was in the shower, so I jumped in with her.

"We need to find you a doctor." I smiled, placing my hand on her stomach.

"I'm going to Cas' doctor on Monday," she stated.

"Good, make sure you let me know the time." Kissing her lips, I truly missed being like this with her. We still have a lot of issues to work out, and I'm still angry about a lot of things, but I'm not letting her go. Once we were done with our shower, we crawled into her bed and made up for lost time.

Chapter Twenty-One

SHAWN

One Month Later

Shit with Britt and I was getting deep, and I was falling for baby girl. But it seems that she likes to hide shit, and that's a problem for me. Her phone kept going off and I've been sitting here for the last twenty minutes reading messages of her and this nigga Tre going back and forth. He's been threatening her on some bitch shit for weeks, and now I see the pussy ass nigga threatening me. I tried to do the right thing and let that nigga live, but after reading this shit, his ass gone get exactly what the fuck I got coming his way.

The worst part of all of this shit is lil' mama hasn't said a muthafuckin' word. I don't take shit like this lightly, and I damn sure won't be waiting for this nigga to come up in my shit. I'm a different type of nigga ain't no waiting, and it damn sure ain't gone be no talking. When you want a snake to die, you cut that bitch off at the head, and that's what's about to happen to this nigga. I heard the water turn off, and I waited for her ass to come out of the bathroom. As soon as she opened the door, I was in her face.

"Why the fuck didn't you tell me this nigga was threatening you and me!" I roared; I was mad as hell.

"I was going to talk to you about it, I swear I was going to tell you. I just thought that I could handle it on my own," she spoke, and her phone started going off.

"Answer your phone."

"It's Kelly, I can call her back. I'm sorry, Shawn, I promise I wasn't trying to hide anything from you. I just didn't want to get you involved in my mess. At first, I thought he was just pissed and just talking shit. But he kept going and when he started going in on you. I knew it was more to it." She wrapped her arms around me, trying to calm me, and her phone was going off again, so she picked it up.

"Hey, Kelly." The look on her face let me know that something was wrong.

"What's up?" I asked her.

"What! We will be on the first flight out." Tears began falling down her face and she broke down.

"I need to know what's going on, lil' mama." I couldn't sit here and watch her cry and she not tell me what happened.

"Somebody set our shop on fire. All that we have worked so hard to build, and they burned down our shit! I have to call Tiff and get flights to LA."

"Fuck! I need to make sure my mom is good, and I'm

coming with you. I got a fuck nigga to deal with, you're getting threatened, and then all of a sudden, y'all shit is set on fire. Nah, that's no coincidence." I called my brother while she was on the phone talking to Tiff. I was pissed, but now I felt bad for yelling at her.

"Sup, bro?"

"Yo, are you home with Tiff?" I asked him.

"I'm pulling in the driveway now. What's going on?"

"Somebody set their damn store on fire. Britt is on the phone with her now, and they're leaving asap to get to LA," I said to him.

"Let me hit up Nas and get the information for the private jet. Y'all get your shit together and come on over. I should have everything set up by the time you get here." I don't know who this nigga thought he was fuckin' with, but he will soon find out it was the wrong move to make.

"It's going to be alright, babe. Pack your bag so we can get out of here." I kissed her lips and went into my closet to get my shit together. About an hour later, we pulled up to my brother's crib, and a few minutes later, they were walking out. When we got to the airport, we were all surprised to see Nas and Priest.

"What are you guys doing here?" Tiff asked.

"You should've known we were coming. We need to know who the hell would do some shit like this to you. Your ex better pray that he didn't have shit to do with this." Priest pulled her in for a hug.

"I'm here to put a hot one in a nigga or two." Nas crazy ass pulled the clip back on his gun as we all boarded the plane.

"Was the fire deliberate or was it some sort of malfunction?" Priest asked.

"We don't know anything; we haven't spoken to anybody other than Kelly, and she was so upset about it we couldn't get anything out of her. I'm glad it's early enough for us to talk to someone when we get there," Britt stated as she got comfortable in her seat.

"I have a bad feeling about this. For some reason, I think someone set our place on fire. I'm just thankful that our workers wasn't in the building." I had to agree with Tiff on that.

"We will get to the bottom of it, believe that!" Cannon said to her.

"I reached out to Big John; he said he ready if we need him," Nas told Cannon.

"Why the hell haven't we taken off yet?" Priest questioned.

"Y'all thought you were going to leave without me?" Kash spoke as he boarded the flight.

"What the hell are you doing here, and where is stepmama? Please don't tell me y'all getting a divorce? This the second time she done let you out of the house. This is going a lil' too far. She knows you leaving the state?" Nas looked at him, and we all fell out laughing.

"When you called and told me what happened, I had to

make this trip. It seems that somebody got a problem with my family and we gone solve that shit for them," Kash spoke, and when Big Kash comes out, it's definitely gone be some problems.

It was going on five in the evening by the time we made it to LA, and we went straight to the girl's shop. Getting out of the trucks, we couldn't believe this shit. The store was burned down to the ground. Tiff and Britt were so heartbroken and full of tears.

"Tiff, Britt, I will give you the money to rebuild. I'm grateful that it's the shop and not either of you. All of this is replaceable, so stop worrying and let's figure out your next move." Priest hugged his cousin, and a few minutes later, the Fire Chief pulled up. Britt called him and he said that he would meet us out here. Priest walked over with the ladies to talk to the chief while we waited.

"Somebody set it on fire and the recordings were burned. The cameras from next door caught one of the guys when he removed his mask. He showed them a still photo, and the girls said they didn't know him. By the way they looked at each other I think they know and just denied it with him." Priest walked over to fill us in on what was going on.

"As they should, they both know how this street shit goes." Nas shrugged.

"We need to get out of here. Whoever did this shit knew that it would bring them back to Los Angeles. And if that's the case, they had to know we were coming with them." What my brother said made sense. Once the girls were done, we went to go check into our hotel.

"The picture he showed us was my ex-boyfriend's brother. So, I know it was him that set this shit up. Urggghhhhh, I'm so pissed at myself," Britt cried.

"You didn't know he would take it this far, Britt, and I'm not going to let you blame yourself. I just wish you would have told us sooner that he was threatening you," Tiff said to her, wrapping her arms around her friend.

"I say we handle this shit and be ready to head back to Philly tonight. The girls can stay in the hotel until we get back." Nas was on the same page as me. I need this nigga dead because a nigga like that ain't gone just stop at burning a building down. You bold enough to do this shit and send the girl threats. I know his bitch ass was sending a message, and I got that shit loud and clear. Priest stayed at the hotel with the ladies, and the rest of us went to the address that Brittany gave us on ole boy.

"What's the plan?" Nas asked as I screwed the silencer on my gun.

"I don't have a plan," I told him and jumped out of the car. It took my brother a couple of minutes to get the door open, and we moved inside the house.

"Bae, you want something to drink?" I heard a girl call out, and as soon as she came into view, Nas grabbed her, putting his gun to her head.

"I'm good!" He yelled out. The closer I got, I could hear him talking, and I assumed he was on the phone.

"I'm sure that hoe knows her shit gone by now..." He stopped talking when I stepped into the room. He tried reaching for his gun, and I lit his ass up. There was no need for me to say shit to that nigga. I heard his girl screaming and cursing about her man. I walked up front where they were, sending two shots to her head. She was riding for her nigga, so I thought it was a good idea for her to join him. No faces, no cases is always my muthafuckin' motto.

Chapter Twenty-Two

BRITTANY

Three months later

It has been a long three months; it was hard for me to bounce back after learning that our store was completely gone. Thank God we had insurance, and that covered just about everything we lost. Cannon and Shawn surprised Tiff and me with a building so that we could rebuild here in Philadelphia. Shawn has been really good to me, and I felt so bad not telling him that I was getting threats from Tre. I truly didn't think he would act on any of it. I guess he proved his point when he set our shit on fire. I should have just cut shit off with him and left it like that.

"Do you know where my brother is?" Mercedes asked, walking into the living room. This girl was crazy as hell. She came over here last night talking about she wanted to stay because her son kept crying. Like bitch, you're part of the reason he's in pain and crying.

"No, he didn't say where he was going," I said to her and went back to texting Tiff. This girl was working my fuckin nerve with her smart-ass mouth.

"He probably out fuckin' Stacia 'cause he was with her last night. I don't know why you here anyway. You're not even his type," she laughed, sitting down and turning on the television.

"Lil girl, what you not gone do is play in my face. I will beat your muthafuckin' ass in here, and I don't care who sister you are. Go play with another bitch before you find my damn fist down your throat," I told her.

"I'm not afraid of you, hoe! You think you special 'cause you fuckin' my brother, bitch. You not the only one he fuckin'! Stupid ass bitch!" She yelled and threw the remote, hitting me in the face. I jumped clean across the table he had in front of the couch to beat that ass. I tried to bury my foot in that hoe neck. The fuck this bitch thought she was playing with.

"Britt!" I heard Shawn yell, lifting me off of his sister.

"Stupid ass bitch talk yo shit now!" I screamed.

"Shawn, kick her ass out. I heard her telling this dude where you hang out at and I asked her about it. She jumped on me when I told her I would tell you, and she started hitting me in the face!" She yelled, and I was confused as hell.

"What! Bitch, you're lying. I didn't tell nobody shit. This bitch been in here running her mouth about you being out with your ex Stacia and then hit me in the face with that damn remote, and that's the reason she got her ass beat." I didn't know what this bitch angle was, but her brother was sitting here listening to her ass.

"How the fuck do I know about the niggas from Cali! That's who I caught her talking to about you. She's trying to set you up, bro. She said she knew for a fact that you killed they brother," This bitch said to Shawn and started smiling when he turned to look at me.

"Britt, what the fuck is she talking about? She's right; she has no clue about the shit that went down in Cali! I know damn well none of the guys said anything to her, so you had to be talking to somebody! How the fuck would she know that shit?!" He screamed in my face.

"I don't know how she knows, but I damn sure didn't tell her. And I haven't talked to anybody about you, so you gone believe what the fuck she's saying?" I asked him because this nigga sounded as if he believed her ass.

"You gotta get up out my shit, shorty! If I find out that you talk to them niggas, we got a problem, lil' baby! Get the fuck up out my shit."

"Shawn! Are you seriously kicking me out over this lying ass bitch? You know what? I'm not gone even go off on you because the shit does look and sound crazy. But I thought we were better than that. You said you loved me. Before I get out yo' shit, let me say this. When you find out the truth, keep that same energy and apology shit over here with you and this lying ass hoe!" I tried not to cry, but this shit was unreal.

He was really taking her side, and the smirk on her face caused the rage in me to overflow. I rushed her ass and knocked that shit right off her face. He pulled me off her ass and got up in my face. I can't believe he was doing this shit! I know it sounds fucked up, but I really didn't say shit to anybody. I went into the bedroom and grabbed the duffle bag that was in the closet, my purse, and left out. Once I got down the street, I called Tiff to come and pick me up. I hated to bother her because she was a little over seven months pregnant and was supposed to be on bed rest. Cannon is so overprotective of her, and I knew he would be upset that she was out. I sat on a bench at the park up the street from Shawn's townhouse.

About forty minutes later, Tiff was pulling into the park. I grabbed my things and went to get into the car.

"Brittany, what the hell happened?" She asked, and I filled her in on the shit that went down.

"Are you fucking kidding me?! How in the hell would she know anything about that?" She questioned, and I had no answers for her.

"Tiff, this bitch straight lied, so I know she on some bull-shit. All I know is, I would never set him up. Something with this shit is not right, and I pray no harm comes their way. Just take me to your moms, I already called her, and she said I can stay there. I'm not going to even put you in a situation with Cannon trying to stay at his house. That's his brother and sister, and he will side with them." Tears fell from my eyes because I was hurt. I was really feeling dude. I've been through so much shit, and no matter how good the dick is, you don't have but one time to make me look like a fool. I was willing to give up my shit and come back to Philadelphia to be with him.

Chapter Twenty-Three

NAS

"Ms. Addie, you know you alright with me. This pecan pie needs to be in somebody's restaurant." We were having dinner at Priest's house.

"Thank you, Nasir! That was my grandmother's recipe, and she made it for us all the time when we were growing up," Ms. Addie stated.

"Damn, Tiff, that's your third slice. Slow yo' ass down, that baby got your ass extra greedy. You sure it's only one baby in there?" I asked her ass.

"Nigga, don't curse me like that. I have one baby in here, and that's all I'm having Anything else they can keep. Now that Aniya is trying to walk, she about to wear my ass out," she spoke.

"How did the visit go with her daddy?" I asked.

"It was good, they had her a birthday party. Aniya didn't

even stay with him; she was with her grandmother the entire time. The last time we took her to visit, it was the same thing. It's like he doesn't even care about seeing her and spending time with her. His wife doesn't want him around me and Aniya." There was no way in hell a chick was gone stop me from seeing my kid.

"Well, that's his loss. Baby girl is always gonna be good over here. Why Britt didn't come?" I knew she was going through it with Shawn.

"The last couple of days have been hard for her. Something is up with Mercedes; you know Britt wouldn't do nothing like that. And Ms. B said she's been partying, drinking and not checking on Jeremiah at all," she stated.

"I spoke to Britt last night, and she told me what went down. She said the girl knew way more than what she should have known. We all know that she didn't get it from Brittany, so her brothers need to find out where she got it from. 'Cause if something happens to my husband, I'm killing me a hoe!" Bear spoke, getting all damn hype.

"Bear, stop all that damn moving around before you make my baby dizzy." I laughed.

"So, how are things with you and Cannon, Tiff?" Zoey asked her.

"Everything is good; we haven't made anything official. We're just waiting to see if the baby is his or not. We were going to get the test done before I delivered. There were risks with it, and Cannon didn't want to do anything to harm the baby." Tiff may not think shit is official, but in Cannon's crazy-ass mind, shit was official when he kicked Dena's ass out.

"Chile, yo' ass been over there falling on the D for months. That's your man, and you just haven't figured that part out yet. That boy done probably got your ass twisted up in new positions over there. I know how you feel, 'cause Joe and me done found us a few new positions. I'mma have to tell you girls about it on our next girl's night so you can try them out," Big Mama laughed, and I almost threw up in my damn mouth.

"Ma!" Pop yelled out, and all the ladies were laughing and cheering her ass on.

"Big ma, don't nobody want to hear that shit! I can't even unsee that bullshit now. Mr. Joe gone have to give me a fair one for poking on my grandma!" Everybody burst out laughing, but I didn't see shit funny.

"Zoey, when is Priest coming back?" Tiff asked her.

"Tomorrow, and I can't wait. Tiff, are you sure that you don't want a baby shower?" Zoe asked, pouting.

"We have everything he needs; Cannon comes home with something different every damn day." She smiled, I'm glad they found a way to work shit out.

"I was going to wait until Priest got back, but I think this is a good time to let you all know that Eva and I are having a baby." I know this nigga fuckin' lying!

"Lawd gone and take me now! This chile done lost his damn mind. What the hell is in the damn water y'all asses drinking? Everybody pregnant! I'm gone start bringing my own damn food and water 'cause me and Joe ain't got time to be pushing out no babies." Big Mama shook her head.

"Pop, I know damn well yo' old ass didn't get my step-mama pregnant. What the hell were y'all old asses thinking! Nigga, when yo' kid turns eighteen you gone have one ass cheek in the grave already. Hell nawl! How me and Priest gone look taking that lil' nigga out introducing him as our lil' brother? Nigga, we gone be thirty plus years apart! It should be against the law for old people to have kids. Cas, take me home; I'm stressed the hell out and grab the rest of the pecan pie. I need that shit for my discomfort. Stepmama, congratulations, but stop letting this nasty nigga shoot up the spot!" I was distraught about that shit. I guess I had to be happy for their old nasty asses. I was gone wait and let his ass tell Priest when he got back. This is some shit that nigga need to know now, so I dialed his number.

"What's up, bro?" He answered on the first ring.

"Yo daddy and stepmama got something to tell you," I told him and passed Pop the phone.

"Hey, son, I just announced to the family that Eva and I are having a baby," Pop spoke, it took a couple minutes for Priest ass to respond.

"Congrats, to you both. I guess I have to prepare myself of become another big brother. I'm sure he or she will be an angel, compared to when you and mom made me a big brother for the first time," He said to Pop and everyone burst out laughing. I snatched my phone from Pop and hung up on his hatin ass. I'm the best lil brother that nigga gone ever have.

"Congrats, Eva and Pop! Don't pay my baby no mind. He just mad that he won't be the baby anymore," Cas laughed, getting up to hug them.

"Congratulations, you two. I pray I make it to see my grandbaby grow up," Big Mama stated.

"Big ma, you gone have to pray a little harder on that request. You might do better praying to see the lil' nigga turn two. 'Cause, thanks to your nasty ass son, you might be gone to glory by the time his lil' ass graduates kindergarten," I blurted, and Cas hit me on the arm. After I got Cas home, I decided to go meet up with Cannon and Shawn down North Philly. When I pulled up, they were on the block talking to Brock.

"Sup?" I spoke, dapping them up.

"Shit! What's going on with you, big brother?" Cannon burst out laughing. I assumed he talked to Tiff ole funky ass because she thought that was the funniest shit ever.

"Fuck you!" I spat.

"My bad, bro. That shit funny as hell, though," his ass laughed.

"Bruh, you still fucked over that shit with you and Britt?" I asked Shawn because his ass looked like he was ready to snap off at any time.

"I'm not fucked up over shit! She had to be on some snake shit because my sister wouldn't know shit about Cali!" He spoke.

"Look, I'm not gone tell you how to feel 'cause that's y'all baby sister. However, my family has been rocking with Brittany a long time, and we stand behind her because we trust her. So, when it comes to her, we gone be at odds. I'm gone always rock with you; I'm just not rocking with you on that shit. Snakes can slither and hide behind anything, including faces." I would hate to get into some shit with him over Britt because I believed what she was saying, and I also believe that Cedes got some foul shit going on.

"Like I told this dude, we can't explain how Cedes found out about it. The fact that she does know have my antennas up, and I'm looking at both of them with a side-eye right now. I will get to the bottom of it, and when I do, we will deal with it accordingly," Cannon spoke, and I had to respect his response. But I'm looking at they sister with the side-eye, which is why I got Cam looking into some shit for me.

Chapter Twenty-Four

BRITTANY

Two **Weeks Later**

"Brittany, get up and get dressed, you're going to this cookout with me. I don't give a damn who's gonna be there," Ms. Gabby fussed. Everyone is going over to Tiff and Cannon's house for a cookout, and I wanted no parts of that shit. I knew that Shawn and his family would be there, and if somebody say something to me, I'mma chin check they ass, and that includes his bitch ass. So, the best thing for me to do is to stay the fuck away from them. I want Tiff to enjoy her last couple of weeks before the baby comes, and I damn sure didn't want to cause any added stress to her. Marlo has been giving her a hard-enough time as it is about Aniya.

"Ms. Gabby, I don't want to stress Tiff out. Because I know if they say something to me, it's gone be a problem," I told her.

"It ain't a problem my .380 can't handle. I don't have anything against them, but Shawn better not bring his lil' young, fine, pretty teeth ass up in there starting no shit. If they on some cool shit, we gone be on some cool shit. If they on that bout it-bout it shit, then we gone be some No Limit fuckin' soldiers up in that bitch tonight. I got you. I told yo' mama on her death bed that I would always watch out for you and that's what the hell I'm gone do.

Now, come on so I can go get my drink on and meet up with my man later." I got up and got dressed because she wasn't taking no for an answer. A couple of hours later, we were pulling up to Cannon's house, and you could hear the music and laughter coming from the back of the house. Ms. Gabby and I walked into the house, and it was definitely going to be hard for me to keep my shit together. The first person I spotted was this hoe ass bitch Mercedes. I'm glad that Cas and Zoey were here. I walked up, giving them a hug.

"Hey, boo. Don't you look cute," Cas stated.

"Thank you, sis. That baby got you glowing, I'm so excited for you and Nas," I spoke just as Tiff came walking into the living room.

"I thought I was gone have to come over to moms and drag your ass out of the house. Just because you know Shawn might be at a family function shouldn't stop you from coming here. You're my family, and if I have to be in this house, you're welcome here just like his damn brother. I'm gone always ride for you," Tiff stated, and I smiled. I appreciate how everyone supported me in this situation, including Priest and Nas. I was surprised when Nas came over a few nights ago to see if I needed anything.

"Britt, everything is going to work out for you. I went through something similar with my husband, and I'm gone tell you we had to fight to get back in a good space with each other. We're all here if you need us. Hopefully, they will find the truth, and Shawn comes around," Zoey spoke. I don't give a damn if his ass comes around or not; he can kiss my ass. I don't ever want to be in a relationship where I have to wonder if you're going to trust what the hell I'm saying. This nigga out here making it look like I'm setting niggas up. Fuck that dude! I'm planning on going back to California and reopening a shop there. I have money saved up and I know Tiff would be down. Once we get the Philadelphia store operational, then we can figure out Cali. Mercedes was mugging the shit out of me, and I felt it in my spirit that I was gonna have to put my fist down this hoe throat before the night was over.

"Y'all lets go out back. I want a burger, and I'm sick of looking at this girl." Cas greedy ass was always trying to eat. Her and Nas were made for each other. As soon as we got outside, I locked eyes with Shawn, and his face was balled up. I guess he was pissed that I was there, and it was nothing he could do about it. I walked up and spoke to the guys while his ass stared me down.

"What's up, Britt? It's been a minute," Cam spoke. It's been a couple of years since I've seen him.

"Hey, Cam. It's good to see you," I spoke and greeted the rest of the guys.

"Britt, you good?" Nas questioned.

"Yeah, I'm doing good."

"Hey, Brittany. I have been trying to call you for the past couple of weeks," Ms. Brenda spoke, walking up to us.

"I'm sorry, Ms. B. I have been getting myself together." I saw her calls; I just didn't want to disrespect her if she started taking up for her son and daughter.

"Yo, bro, I'm out of here. I can't be around fraud ass people," Shawn said to his brother, and I wanted to punch this nigga in his fuckin face.

"Nigga, chill the fuck out with all that shit! I told your ass what side of the fence I'm riding for and why I'm doing it. So, you need to think about what you gone say out your mouth. This girl ain't did shit to you, and deep down, I think you know that shit. You need to really evaluate the source that you got that information from."

"Whew, chile! That nigga would have my whole foot in his ass," Cas said, shaking her head.

"Nah, fuck him! He can believe his sister; all I know is they better leave my name out they fuckin' mouth!" I yelled in his face.

"Get the fuck out my face," he gritted as he stepped closer to me.

"Britt, come talk to me for a second." Cam grabbed my hand, pulling me away from him.

"This don't have shit to do with you, bruh," Shawn said to Cam.

"You need to find a place to channel that anger. I'm not

the channel your ass should be on. I'm gone let you rock out cause you look stressed." Cam chuckled as he grabbed my hand and pulled me away with him. All we heard was Shawn going the fuck off, calling me names, and talking shit about Cam.

"This shit is getting out of fuckin' hand! That lil' girl almost made me smack the shit out of her. The whole time y'all were arguing, she was smiling. Something is up with that lil' evil, troll ass lookin lil' bitch. I think her brothers stole all the looks and left that bitch with a touch of ugly. Funny looking hoe! Lawd, I don't feel like going to jail, but I will proudly sit up in that bitch until y'all bail me out. I need to go home and get high, 'cause this drink ain't doing shit for me," Ms. Gabby fussed.

"Yeah, y'all need to keep an eye on her. I'm looking into some stuff, and I will keep you up to date," Cam spoke, shaking his head at the foolishness.

"They lucky I'm pregnant, I swear when this baby drop, I'm beating her ass. And I'm gone fuck Shawn ass up for believing her. I don't give a fuck about her being their sister, fuck that hoe!" Tiff was going off as she walked up to us. I guess something went down because she was mad as hell.

"Tiff, you need to calm the fuck down," Cannon told her as he came out front.

"Nah, you need to get your disrespectful ass brother and sister the fuck out of here. They not gone be fuckin' with my friend. She didn't say shit to them, yet they want to call her out her fuckin' name," Tiff spat.

"That's still my brother and sister, just like Britt is your friend!" He yelled, and as soon as Tiff tried to respond, she was bent over screaming in pain.

"Tiff! What's wrong?" Cannon asked her.

"My water broke!" She screamed. Cannon wasted no time getting her into the car and pulling out of the driveway. Zoey took Aniya home with her, and Ms. Gabby and I went to the hospital. After my best friend haves her baby, I think its best that I go back to California.

Chapter Twenty-Five

CANNON

iff and I were preparing for this day. We thought we had a few more weeks to get things set up. She's been under a lot of pressure due to Aniya's bitch ass daddy. Tiff asked me not to fuck with his ass, for Aniya's sake. I loved that little girl as if she were my own, and I didn't want her hurt off of some shit that I caused. I promised her mother that I would back up and let her deal with that nigga. Tiff and I haven't talked about being in a relationship. She wanted to wait until the baby was born to figure out the rest. She could take all the time she needs. As far as I'm concerned, we in this shit until my fuckin' casket drop. I'm not feeling this shit with Shawn and Brittany. I'm trying to understand my brother's logic behind this bullshit.

I just don't know if I believe what the hell Cedes is saying. Her ass is still on some fuck shit when it comes to Jeremiah and helping my mom take care of him. He is paralyzed from the waist down, and if I could bring that nigga back from the dead, I would just to murder his ass all over again. Jeremiah's dad is in jail doing a bid, and his family don't think that's his son. So, they don't want anything to do with him.

"Cannon! It hurts so bad!" Tiff cried.

"Tiff, you're the one that wanted to have the baby naturally. Do you want them to give you something for the pain?" I asked her, and I was amazed that she even wanted to have a natural birth.

"No, I don't want it. It took me twenty hours to have Aniya and I heard that those medications kind of slows everything down. I just want this little boy out of me," she spoke.

"I know, baby girl." I rubbed her body down, trying to make her feel better. About ten minutes later, Dr. Long walked into the room. She tried to get Cas's doctor, but I wanted her to have a woman doctor, so we ended up using his partner.

"Tiffany, I need to check to see how far you've dilated," she spoke, and Tiff was in so much pain all she could do was nod.

"Just try to breathe through the pain, baby, and pretty soon, it will all be over," Ms. Gabby told her.

"Oh my God! I can't take this shit! Please get him out of me!" She screamed. I began kissing her lips and face, trying to soothe her.

"Ok, Tiffany, on the next contraction, I want you to start pushing," Dr. Long told her.

"Ok...Urghhhhhhhhh!" she screamed as she began to push.

"Good job, Tiffany. We're going to do the same thing on the next contraction." Dr. Long was so laid back, and I guess you would be when you do this shit all the time. But a nigga stomach was feeling a little queasy.

"Ohhhh my God! He's coming out, I can feel him!" She cried, I peeped over to see what the doctor was doing, and that was the wrong move. I almost passed the fuck out.

"You got this, baby," Ms. Gabby spoke, holding her daughter's hand.

"His head is out. On this next one, give me a big push." Tiff did what she said and pushed baby boy right on out. My heart felt like it was going to jump out of my chest when I laid eyes on him.

"Dad, you can cut the cord now." I prayed for this kid to be my child. I sure hope God answered my prayers.

"Awww, he is so handsome, baby," Ms. Gabby cried, looking over at her grandson.

"Here is your beautiful bundle. He weighs Seven pounds even, and he's nineteen inches long," The nurse spoke, placing him into his mother's arms.

"He is perfect." Tiff smiled, admiring her son. After all that we've been through, this moment made things so much better. I couldn't love this girl more than I loved her right now. Watching her bring life into this world was a beautiful thing, and I will never forget this moment. After they got Tiff squared away, the family came in so that they could see the baby. My brother and sister wasn't here. My mom said she told them it was best not to come right now. I hate that Shawn was in this position because he was excited about this, possibly being my son. Nas sent me a text letting me know that they would see us tomorrow.

"He is a beautiful baby," my mom said as she admired him.

"Thank you, Ms. Brenda." She smiled.

"Look at him, my godson is so adorable. You did good, friend. I'm so happy for you," Britt told her as she placed the baby back in her arms. The nurse took the baby to the nursery to get cleaned up and said she would bring him back soon. Tiff was going to breastfeed him, so he would be spending most of his time in the room with his mother.

"Baby, I'm going to get out of here and let you get some rest. Brittany is not feeling too well, and I want to get her back to the house. I will be back in the morning to see you before I go pick up Aniya from Zoey." Ms. Gabby kissed her daughter, and Brittany said her goodbyes as well.

"I'm going to leave you two alone and get Jeremiah from Shawn's house. Bry, as soon as you have time, we need to sit down and have a talk with that boy. I don't like the way he's going about all of this mess with Brittany," my mom said to me. She gave Tiff and I a hug and left.

"You did good, lil' mama," I said, kissing her lips and rubbing my fingers through her hair. She looked exhausted, and I'm glad everyone left so she could get some rest.

"Thank you, I guess we need to name him," she sighed.

"Yeah, I'm going to leave that up to you." I knew it would take some time to get the DNA test results back, and to be honest, I just wanted to enjoy our son. No matter what, the results were, that little boy is my son.

———

*T*hree weeks later

Life is good! I have the woman that stole my heart back in my life and the DNA results came back that Lil Bry was my son. Tiff and I named him Bryshere Kalil Mason, and I loved the hell out of my lil' dude. Shawn and I were on our way to our moms to check on her and our nephew. We agreed to be more hands-on to help her with him, so every other weekend, Shawn and I take turns getting him so that mom can have some time to herself. Mercedes is just a lost cause. We tried talking to her, but she's still doing the same dumb shit. Disrespecting our mom and giving her son her ass to kiss.

"How is Tiff doing?" Shawn asked. Tiff don't fuck with him because of the shit that went down with Brittany.

"She's good, she's not feeling the fact that Britt left and went back to Cali." I looked over at him, and he seemed to be in deep thought. I pulled into the gas station to get some gas.

"You want something out of the store?" Shawn asked.

"Nah, I'm good." We both got out the car, and I pumped the gas while he went inside the store. My phone was going off, and I pulled it out to answer it.

"What's up, ma?"

"Bry, y'all need to be careful and get over here. I overheard your sister on the phone with some guy, and I think she's the one setting your brother up," she spoke.

"What!" I gritted.

"From what I heard, they have been watching Shawn for days and I heard her say something about y'all being at a gas..."

"Who the fuck are you talking to?" I heard Mercedes scream at my mom.

"Mercedes, I'm your mother! Put that fucking gun down!" My mom screamed, and the call dropped. Just as I tried to call her back, I heard screeching tires roll up when I saw them jump out on my brother with guns pushing him in the truck. I pulled my shit out and started busting on them niggas. They started shooting back as they sped the fuck off!

"Fuckkkkkkk!" I roared, running back to my car, speeding out of the parking lot trying to catch these niggas, and a fuckin' car crashed into me. They might as well get ready 'cause I'm killing every nigga that touched my fuckin' brother!

Chapter Twenty-Six
TIFF

"Have you talked to Britt?" My mom asked.

"Yeah, I talked to her a few weeks ago. She's been a little distant, and I think she's really going through it. Cannon said Shawn has been walking around mad at the world, and I think it's because he knows he messed up by believing Mercedes. I miss my friend, and as soon as I can travel, I'm going to spend some time with her. Maybe we can go on a little girl's trip," I said to my mom.

"That sounds nice, I think she would love that. You know I'm overprotective of you girls, and I don't like the way she was treated by him. One thing about Britt is I know she's going to bounce back. I don't know if Shawn is going to be able to fix this shit with her, Britt doesn't forgive easily." My mom was right about that. It took a lot of work for Tre to even get her to speak to his ass again after he cheated on her.

The kids and I were on our way home from my mom's house. I had to damn near fight my daughter to get her to come home with me. That little girl loved her grandmother and my mom loved her. I loved the bond that the two of them have with each other. My phone was going off, and I thought it was Cannon calling me back, but it was from an unknown number.

"Hello...Hello..." I had been getting these calls for a few weeks now. Things with Marlo was getting out of hand because he didn't want Aniya around Cannon. And wants a DNA test done on Bryshere. I tried to explain that we already had a DNA test done, and Cannon is Bry's dad. I don't even know why he's so pressed he doesn't even want to spend time with Aniya. Marlo's mom told me that his wife doesn't want Aniya at their house, and I swear I was ready to beat that bitch's ass again.

Cannon and I took her to California a couple of times to see her family, and his ass barely spent any time with her. He was so hell-bent on his beef with Cannon, and the only reason Cannon hasn't reacted is because of me asking him not to. I can't believe how things have changed for us, and I was loving every minute of it. Cannon is so in love with Niya, and he adores his son. I'm so happy to see him happy.

Pulling into the garage, I jumped out of the car because Bry was screaming at the top of his lungs. I got him and Niya out of the car so that I could get them into the house. I decided to come back for the rest of my things after I got them situated. As soon as I got them in their rooms, my phone was going off. I saw that it was Britt and I was so excited to hear from her.

"Hey, boo! How are you?" I asked her.

"I'm doing alright, I had to take some time and regroup, but I'm good. How are my god babies?" I was mad as hell that she left and didn't say anything to us. She did leave a note for my mom explaining why it was best that she move back to California. I felt bad for her, but she had to do what was best for her, and I couldn't be selfish about it.

"They're so perfect, and things are going good with Cannon and me. I can't believe that we're together with a son. Britt, when it comes to us, he's so soft and hands-on with the kids, I loved that about him," I said to her.

"That's good to hear, friend. I'm so happy for you. I hope God blesses you with your heart's desire. Kelly and Janelle are helping me find a store location, and I will let you know as soon as we got something. Kelly and I will be there to help you open up the Philly store when you're ready." I could hear the sadness in her voice, and my heart broke for her that things didn't work out with her and Shawn because she loved that man.

"Ok, that sounds great. Let me call you back in a few. I need to get a shower while the kids are quiet." I laughed because my son don't play about getting his milk.

"Ok, give the kids kisses for me, and I will talk to you later." Britt and I hung up, and I went to take my shower. As soon as I turned the shower off, I could hear my phone ringing. I ran into the bedroom to grab it, and I missed Cannon's call. I dialed him back and he picked up.

"Tiff I need you to get the kids and go over to Nas and Cas' house until you hear from me!" He yelled into the phone.

"What's wrong, baby?" I didn't like the way he sounded.

"Tiff, just go and go now! These niggas done grabbed my fuckin brother, and something is going on with my mom. Get my kids out of there and go to Nas' house now!" He yelled and hung up.

What the fuck is going on? Who the fuck would take Shawn?

I threw some clothes on and ran into Aniya's room to get her. I could hear Bry crying, but my steps were halted when I walked into his room. This crazy bitch Dena was sitting in my chair breastfeeding my fuckin' son. She looked as if she was about six months pregnant, and her gun was pointed at me!

To Be Continued

CPSIA information can be obtained
at www.ICGtesting.com
Printed in the USA
LVHW021540061120
670969LV00010B/1043

9 798682 646104